THE ORPHAN PRODIGY'S STOLEN TALE

RACHEL DOWNING

CORNERSTONETALES.COM

CHAPTER 1

Isabella Farmerson had no idea that her life would change forever on her tenth birthday. Obviously, she knew that the day was a momentous day. She would now have two digits in her age - a fact she was incredibly excited about - but this day of celebration would end in mourning, loss and grief.

The morning had started out with a surprise breakfast with her father and mother Oscar and Lucy. A large chocolate cake sat in the centre of the dining table, which made Isabella's small eyes bulge in delight. She was never allowed cake for breakfast!

"Well, my dear little one," her father said, a gleam in his eye. "Today must be a very special day." He turned to her mother. "I was quite sure it was a special day, but now, I can't seem to remember why. Can you Lucy?"

Isabella's mother put a finger to her chin, and tapped it, presenting the look of being deep in thought. "You know, now that you mention it… No! It has completely slipped my mind."

Isabella giggled at her parents antics. They had always been very affection towards her. Her mother called her 'my little gift', as they had been trying for many years to have a child, without any luck. They had almost given up, when Isabella had been conceived and was born. Around the same time, Oscar's career began to take off too, and he was now a managing supervisor in a factory. "Got to make sure I can always look after my girls," he would say as he'd pull Isabella into a bear hug. Being a supervisor meant he would have to spend many hours working, and with Isabella getting teaching from her governess, it could have been very easy that the three of them wouldn't get to spend much time together, but Oscar and Lucy always made sure to find times for family, just like now.

"I'm sure it must be something..." Oscar continued the charade. "For look, there's a cake on the breakfast table!"

"A cake on the breakfast table!" Lucy said with mock surprise. "But cake can only be for breakfast on people's tenth birthdays. Is it your tenth birthday husband?"

Isabella was almost wholly overcome with giggles, but she let out with a shrill squeal, "No! It's my tenth birthday!" After doing so, she collapsed to the floor with joyous laughter. Her mother and father came over and embraced her, kneeling down to do so.

"Happy birthday, my little gift." Isabella's mother nuzzled her nose in Isabella's hair affectionately. "It takes my breath away to see how much you've grown."

"But you'll always be our little girl." Her father gently interjected. "Always."

Isabella hugged both of them, squeezing as tightly as she could. She knew she was so incredibly blessed to have such loving parents.

"Now," her father said, "I believe that cake needs to be eaten quickly, or else it might get stale. Do you agree, Isabella?" Isabella nodded enthusiastically. She more than agreed.

∼

EVEN THOUGH IT was her birthday, that didn't mean Isabella could simply shirk off her teachings for the day. Her governess Mrs Paxton, however, had conceded to make the day a fun trip out. Sometimes Mrs Paxton's understanding of fun was very different from Isabella's, but today it seemed to line up, because she had organised a trip for the two of them to the Zoo in Regent's Park. Isabella wasn't aware of how tricky it was to get a ticket - the zoo was in such high demand - but that was one of the perks of Oscar's business position; he was able to pull some strings and procure the tickets.

Still buzzing from the rush of sugar the breakfast of soft spongey cake had given, Isabella had to refrain herself from simply sprinting swiftly ahead of Mrs Paxton.

"C'mon c'mon c'mon!" She implored.

"No need to rush, little one." Mrs Paxton said with a chuckle. "The cages are there for a reason. The animals aren't going anywhere."

This stopped Isabella in her tracks. "How did all the animals get to zoo, Miss?"

Mrs Paxton let out a breath, giving her time to think. "I would say they all came to the zoo in different ways and for different reasons."

"They all have their own stories. Their own tales of their travels." Isabella felt the weight of that thought on her mind.

"And some even have tails too!" Mrs Paxton jested. Isabella giggled at her wit. "Come along! Let's spend your birthday doing the best thing."

"And what is the best thing?" Isabella asked, already knowing the answer. This was somewhat of a routine for the two of them.

"Learning!" Mrs Paxton said with a smile.

Isabella wasn't sure if she entirely agreed with Mrs Paxton's sentiment about learning, but the zoo was most definitely an utter joy. She loved seeing all of the different animals, some rather pedestrian, and some she didn't even know existed until she saw them with her own eyes. Mrs Paxton made sure to read out all the facts listed about each animal, but Isabella only paid half-attention to all that. The thing she loved most was looking into each animal's eye, and trying to work out what their story was, what their name and their dreams were. Her daydreams spiraled in her head, leaving her mind full of fantastical stories of adventurers, grand escapes and even grander rescues. They played out like the greatest puppet shows in her imagination as they walked back home at the end of the day. The sun was only just starting to dip behind the buildings.

When they rounded the corner to their street, Isabella instantly noticed that a lot of people were standing outside their house. Some of them she recognised as neighbours, but others she'd never seen before. Quite a few seemed to be dressed in uniforms: police uniforms.

"Miss?" Isabella felt tiny. She didn't feel like a grown-up ten year old anymore. "What's going on?"

"I'm not sure." Mrs Paxton took Isabella's hand, as they cautiously approached the crowd. "Just stick with me. I'm sure everything is fine."

Everything was not fine. Isabella could feel it. In fact, she was sure that things were about as far from fine as they could be.

And she was right.

CHAPTER 2

"It happened very fast." The policeman switched his gaze between Mrs Paxton and Isabella periodically, talking to them both. "People caught glimpses of the culprit, so we have a working description to go off of."

The culprit. Isabella hadn't heard that word before, but she could guess what it meant. The culprit was the person who had done this. The culprit was the person who had broken into their house, not even an hour ago, had ransacked the place, and had left her mother and father lying on the floor, their lives stolen from them. The culprit was the person who had stolen her family from her.

Isabella hadn't been allowed into the house, but she had broken free of Mrs Paxton's grip and slipped her way through both neighbours and policemen. She caught a glimpse of her parents on the kitchen floor, their faces whiter than any she had ever seen. A police man – Mr Fulham – had grabbed her and led her away as quickly as he could. It was too late though. She had seen enough.

She was now sitting on the sofa in the living room. Mrs Paxton had done her best to prepare some tea for the police as well as Isabella. Isabella sat wrapped in her bed's blanket; it was to help with the shock she was told. Maybe the shock was the reason she couldn't really feel anything at all.

Her parents were dead. She knew that. She had been told it, and she had seen them. But she couldn't accept it in her heart yet. They had just this morning been dancing around the room with chocolate smeared on their faces. They can't be gone.

Mrs Paxton put a hand on Isabella's head, though Isabella did not react to it. "Thank you Mr Fulham. I think we can save the details around the little one." Mr Fulham nodded in agreement, an apologetic look on his face. What was he sorry for? It wasn't his fault. It was the culprits fault. "What happens now?" Mrs Paxton asked.

"Well…" Mr Fulham cleared his throat. "In regards to the house and possessions, that all depends on the legalities and-"

Isabella stopped listening. She wouldn't understand any of it anyways. Instead, she decided to dive back into her daydream she had left behind not even twenty minutes ago, of the different zoo animals and their adventures. She rode atop a tiger, and a paper of zebras - who she had decided would grow wings - flew above her on either side. This make believe world made more sense to her than anything happening in the real one.

"And what about Isabella?" The sound of her name snapped Isabella out of her fantasy. "What happens to her?"

"She'll have to stay with her next of kin." Isabella didn't know what that meant.

"She doesn't have any other family." Mrs Paxton said flatly. Kin must mean family then, Isabella quickly deduced. "And before you ask, I cannot take her in. I am only just getting by myself. Isn't there anything you can do?"

"Then…" Mr Fulham took a moment to consider his words. "If there is no one who can take her in. She'll have to be taken to an orphanage."

"What's an orphanage?" Isabella squeaked.

Mrs Paxton looked to Mr Fulham, but he simply looked down at the floor. She turned to Isabella. "An orphanage is where children who don't have any parents or family go to live and be taken care of."

"Oh..." It was then that it truly started to hit Isabella. She didn't have any parents anymore. She didn't have any family. She didn't even know if she had any belongings. She had nothing.

"You'll make lots of new friends." Mr Fulham said. "Children who are in the same position as you." He winced slightly as his description.

"So... Like a zoo for lost kids?" Isabella asked both adults

There was a slight pause before Mrs Paxton summoned up the fortitude to reply. "Yes, my dear, like a zoo for lost kids."

"And I'm a lost kid now..." Isabella's eyes wandered to the door that led through to the kitchen. Through to that awful sight.

Isabella was given only a couple minutes to go to her room and pack some changes of clothes. Mrs Paxton helped her, doing her best not to cry.

It struck Isabella that she hadn't cried yet. She knew she probably should, but that wave of emotion hadn't hit just yet.

"Only take what you need." Mrs Paxton said pragmatically. "And make sure the clothes are practical." She was basically talking to herself as she alone packed the clothes. Isabella stood staring into space.

"Will I ever see you again, Miss?" Even Isabella was surprised this is what she said.

Mrs Paxton froze with one of Isabella's night shirts in her hand. Her mouth opened, and then closed again. She gently put the shirt down, and knelt down to be at eye level with Isabella.

She stroked one of Isabella's cherub cheeks before speaking. "I won't lie to you, I don't know." Her voice caught in her throat.

She cleared it and tried again. "Your parents were always good to me, Isabella, but I can't live on charity. I have a family of my own to feed and fend for."

"Am I not your family?" Isabella's frowned.

"You..."

Isabella didn't let her finish. Instead, the little girl fell forward into her governess's arms and pulled her into an embrace. Mrs Paxton returned the hug, stroking Isabella's back softly.

"If I don't see you again... Thank you for taking me to the zoo." Isabella's kindness, even in the face of such horror finally broke Mrs Paxton, and she wept.

Mrs Paxton's tears finally let Isabella's feelings break through the dam of shock, and she too cried. She wept and wept, soaking Mrs Paxton's shirt. She didn't know where she would end up, and who she would be with. Just this morning, the fact there was so much she didn't know was exciting, it was all an opportunity to learn. Now, her ignorance was the scariest thing.

CHAPTER 3

Isabella had never heard of the orphanage she was sent to. This wasn't too surprising to her though, as she had never had a reason to even learn what an orphanage was until recently.

It was an all-girls orphanage, which Mr Fulham had promised was the best around. Well, best around for a little girl with nothing to her name. Isabella didn't understand any of the specifics, and no one had even tried to explain them to her, but all of her parent's possessions had been claimed by the company her father had worked for. She had heard mutterings from the adults who were buffeting her around saying things like "stingy businessman" and "literally robbing a child blind", but Isabella couldn't get anyone to actually explain to her what had happened. All she knew for certain was, she had nothing to her name, except the clothes which Mrs Paxton had put into her bag, they had let her keep those.

The orphanage hadn't let her keep them though. The minute she arrived, the woman who ran the place, Miss Strawn, demanded the bag of her.

"You won't be needing any of these." She had said through a

thin mouth that seemed to be in a perpetually frown. "Here, all girls have a uniform. You have two sets, so you can wash one whilst wearing the other. This is to encourage cleanliness amongst the pupils." Miss Strawn had a very funny way of talking about the orphanage as if it was a school, calling the girls pupils, and insisting they follow a tight regimented schedule. Sometimes, it even felt more like an army barracks than a school.

Isabella had been deposited at the orphanage on a Tuesday evening, a mere five days after everything had happened. She had cried with Mrs Paxton, but all the pain was still very fresh. Miss Strawn had been made aware of her position, but did her no charity. She was left alone at the end of her bed - a small stiff mattress in a long line of small stiff mattresses that filled the room - with her two sets of clothes.

"The other girls will be coming back from dinner soon, and you'll get to meet them." Miss Strawn said. Isabella didn't feel like meeting a whole new group of girls, but she didn't have a choice. "Have you eaten, girl?" Isabella shook her head. Mr Fulham had kept her well fed during her short tenure living at the police station, but she hadn't had anything for dinner. "Too bad." Miss Strawn tutted. "If you'd only have arrived earlier, you could have gone for dinner. You'll have to wait for breakfast in the morning now." Isabella chose not to point out that her arrival time had nothing to do with her, she was simply at the mercy of the adults in her life. The adults seemed to be ever changing lately, unlike before, where her parents and Mrs Paxton were solid absolutes. Isabella didn't expect the cold and strict Miss Strawn to be her new foundation.

As soon as Miss Strawn had left the large communal bedroom - it seemed to have been a factory of some kind beforehand and been repurposed - Isabella sat down on the rock hard mattress and started to cry. She done her best to hold it all in during the time of being buffeted about, but now that it looked like she had landed, she felt the weight of it all hit her again. She let the tears flow, not bothering to wipe them from her small cheeks.

"Are you okay?" A sweet little voice surprised Isabella. She looked up, and had to wipe the tears from her eyes to see who had spoken clearly. It was another young girl, who looked about Isabella's age. Though instead the auburn hair that Isabella had, this girl had a dark blonde, and it was cut a lot shorter. In her hand, she held a roll of bread. Isabella's eyes bounced between the girls face and the roll, but she didn't say anything.

The girl held the roll out to her. "I know how Miss Strawn can be. How strict she is about mealtimes, and when I saw you arriving in the cart, I knew she would refuse to make an exception and give you a late dinner, so I swiped this for you." Isabella took the roll thankfully. "I'd eat it up quickly though, the others will be back soon, and someone might snitch."

"Snitch?" Isabella asked in between taking to big bites of the roll. It wasn't the nicest bread, but for an empty stomach, it was better than cake. Isabella pushed away the thought of cake, the memories now associated with it spoilt it entirely.

The girl's face furrowed in thought. "Like... Um... To snitch is to tell on someone. If you see someone doing something they shouldn't and you expose them, even if they weren't hurting anyone."

"You giving me this roll... You're not supposed to do that?" Isabella paused her feasting.

The girl shook her head. "Not by Miss Strawn's rules. But I don't think her rules are very fair, and sometimes, I'd prefer to be a good person, than obey." She smiled mischievously. "I'm Nancy by the way."

"I'm Isabella." Isabella swallowed the last of the roll, just as the sound of many footsteps started echoing down the hall. The other girls were returning from dinner.

"Well Isabella." Nancy put her hands on her hips proudly.

"Would you like for me to be your best friend, and to show you around this place?"

Isabella nodded. "I would very much like that. I... I don't have anyone." She could feel the sting of tears forming in her eyes again.

Nancy sat down beside her on the bed, and put her arm around Isabella. "Don't worry, Izzy. No one here has anyone. Not even Miss Strawn, I think that's why she's so cold. Being lonely doesn't help anyone. But guess what?"

"What?"

"You're not alone anymore. You got me. You got Nancy."

Isabella found herself smiling weakly. Maybe things could be alright, with Nancy there to guide her.

"Right, Izzy." Nancy stood up. "I'm going to go over to my bed now as to not get in trouble, but as soon as the lights are out, I'll sneak right back over."

"No one's ever called me Izzy before."

The first of the girls were coming through the door at the end of the hall now, so Nancy spoke quickly and quietly as she dashed across the room. "That's because you've never known a Nancy before. But now you do!"

Isabella quickly brushed the few crumbs that had ended up on her bed onto the floor, and then kicked them underneath. All the girls who arrived barely gave Isabella a second glance. This probably was a usual occurrence to them, which made Nancy's kindness even more poignant. They all started lining up at the end of the beds, and Nancy motioned that Isabella should do the same. She did so without quite understanding what was going on.

"Right girls." Miss Strawn's voice pierced through any remaining chatter that was occurring, resulting in dead silence. "Inspection time. And for the sake of our new pupil, Isabella, I will explain again what I am searching for." Miss Strawn started to work down the line of girls. The age range surprised Isabella, there appeared to be some as young as four, and some as old as adults, though she seemed to remember a mention of the orphanage only housing up until the age of eighteen. Miss Strawn clutched at the girl's cheeks and pulled their faces upwards towards her to get a clear look at them. "Cleanliness is the most important aspect to a lady. If you are not clean, you cannot be a lady. And if you cannot be a lady…" She paused, waiting.

"Then we shall never find a home that wants us." The chorus droned. Isabella almost jumped in surprise.

Miss Strawn's smile - if you could even call it that - grew for a moment on her face. "Very good girls." The smile disappeared as quickly as it had appeared. She continued her examination down the line. She halted abruptly in front of one of the smallest girls. One of her long slender spider-like fingers scrapped across the girls lower lip. "And what's this, Anastasia?"

Anastasia's lip quivered and she didn't answer.

A cane which Isabella hadn't even noticed Miss Strawn was wielding was raised, and Anastasia put out her tiny palms without a fight. Two loud cracks echoed against the ceiling. None of the other girls, except for Nancy and Isabella, watched.

"I hope I won't have many more I'll need to scold tonight." Miss Strawn said, but Isabella wasn't so sure she was being entirely truthful.

When Miss Strawn passed by Isabella she simply stated. "I hope this gives you an impression as to the kind of operation I run, Isabella." Miss Strawn looked down at the cane. "I don't tolerate laziness of any kind. Do we understand each other?"

"Yes." Isabella could barely get the word out, fear gripped her throat so tightly.

"Yes, what?"

The cane suddenly looked a lot thicker and a lot harder. "Yes… Miss?" Isabella hoped her assumption was right.

It seemed to be, as Miss Strawn nodded in satisfaction and moved along to the next girl.

In total, seven of the twenty-eight girls were scalded with the cane. Fifty-six cracks echoed out. Fifty-six palms were left red and sore after the inspection was done.

The sun had set during the inspection, and the only light left in the hall was coming from a candle at the end of it. As Miss Strawn left, she took the candle with her. Isabella could hear the shuffling of everyone as they climbed into bed, muscle memory making it easy in the dark. She did her best to do the same, only bumping her shin once on the bed frame.

After about ten minutes of laying in the darkness, unable to sleep, the moonlight started to peep through one of the high windows, giving the room a small amount of illumination. Nancy slipped out of bed, as quiet as a mouse, and snuck over to Isabella.

"You okay?" Nancy asked.

"Yes." Isabella whispered back. "Is it always this strict and awful?"

"Sometimes it's worse."

"How do you survive it?"

"The same way anyone survives life when they're dealt a bad hand." Isabella could hear Nancy's grin more than she could actually see it. "One day at a time."

"One day at a time."

Nancy patted Isabella - who was still sat half-covered by her bedsheets - on the back. "And just think of the incredible tale we'll have at the end of all this. How we survived the cruel oppression of the Dread Queen Strawn." The girls had to suppress their giggles. "Izzy the conqueror, has a nice ring to it, don't it?"

"But only if Nancy the fearless is there too." Isabella was so grateful to finally have a kind face that wouldn't disappear within a couple days.

CHAPTER 4

To Isabella's relief, Nancy didn't disappear. She was by Isabella's side as soon as the morning began, which was earlier than Isabella had ever experienced before.

Miss Strawn entered the hall of beds mere moments after the sun had dawned, and rang a large bell to awaken them all. Isabella had already been awake - nightmares had kept her from falling asleep - but the sudden loud clang still made her yelp in surprise. A couple of giggles spattered across the room at the noise Isabella made, but they were quickly shut up as Miss Strawn started striding down the room.

"Who made that noise?" Her voice was filled with an unwarranted fury. "A lady does not yelp."

"I made the noise." Nancy piped up before Isabella could say anything.

Miss Strawn stalked over to Nancy, and without saying anything, the small girl held out her palms. Crack. Crack. Isabella couldn't even look as it happen. Those strikes were meant for her.

The first thing of the rigid schedule was breakfast. As all the girls started trawling out towards the food hall, Nancy came over to Isabella.

"I'm so so sorry!" Isabella said. "I didn't know-"

"No worries." Nancy rubbed her palms, a slight mark had already come up. "Not the first time I've been under Miss Strawn's wrath."

"But it wasn't you. You didn't deserve them."

"No one deserves all this." Nancy said flatly. "I'd rather take on some of it whilst you're learning the ropes at least. Besides." Her eyes gleamed with excitement. "I want to be a real hero when we tell the tale to people."

NANCY DID JUST as she said, and showed Isabella the ropes. After each meal, she helped Isabella clean up both her bowl, dress, and face to make sure they were to Miss Strawn's standards. Between breakfast and lunch, the girls had lessons, which mainly consisted of a very bored looking nun reading passages from both the Bible and an ancient looking textbook whilst all the "pupils" sat in dutiful silence. Isabella did her best to concentrate, after all, learning was the best thing, but the lessons were so dull and the teaching style did nothing to aid that. She found herself drifting off to sleep sometimes, but Nancy would always make sure to give her a rapid tap reaching across from her desk whilst no one was watching.

After lunch - which never felt like enough though Isabella would never give Miss Strawn the satisfaction of being able to scold her for complaining - all the girls got an hour of playtime in a small outside area fenced off by a tall old-looking stone wall. No toys of any kind were provided, or jump rope, or even some chalk to draw a hop-scotch on the ground. They all were simply left to their own devices.

The girls all broke off into their various cliques, mainly

divided by age, though some Isabella would come to discover, decided to group themselves by how they had become an orphan: the "never knows" had never known their parents, the "late bloomers" had become orphans later in life, and the "want nots" had been abandoned by their parents. Isabella was a "late bloomer", but that didn't seem to bother Nancy, who was a "want not".

"It doesn't make sense to me, all that deciding who to like based on who is the same as you." Nancy once mused to Isabella during their playtime. "If we only ever played with people who are like us, how would we ever grow up? We would just stay on the same path all the time." Isabella couldn't agree more. She was so grateful for Nancy.

Nancy never spoke about her life before the orphanage, predominately because she couldn't remember any, but she never begrudged Isabella from telling stories about her parents and Mrs Paxton. If anything, Nancy encouraged her to, enjoying the way Isabella could weave a tale together. Sometimes even, during playtime, as Isabella told a story - perhaps the one about her father accidentally stepping in a puddle of horse manure, or the one about her mother accidentally mending a dress inside out - a small audience of girls would gather around and listen alongside Nancy. Isabella loved it when they did. Nothing felt better than eliciting a chuckle at the perfect point, or knowing your audience is holding their breath in anticipation, and the immense satisfaction when they let it free at the stories climax.

"When we do eventually sell our tale." Nancy said. "I want you to be the one that tells it. You're a natural!"

After their allotted hour of playtime, it was more lessons. These ones were on sewing, mending, cooking, and cleaning, though there never was enough of anything for everyone to get a go. Isabella sometimes got a chance to practise sewing a hemline, or attempt to get a stain out of a shirt, but she never fought for it.

It was also during these practical lesson times that anyone interested in adopting one of the girls could come and meet and talk with them. In all Isabella's time though, she had never once see someone come. Some of the older girls, the ones who were seventeen, said people had come a couple times, but only ever once was a girl adopted.

Adoption was not an escape option for these girls. Their only hope was, once they were cast out at eighteen, that their piratical skills and manners could secure them a job in a factory or as a cleaner quickly enough that they wouldn't become beggars on the street.

Then to conclude the day, dinner. Then bedtime and lights out.

Things ran like clockwork everyday apart from Sundays, where they would all travel a little ways down the street to a church - Isabella believed it might have been the church the teacher nun was a part of - and attend morning mass. It was on these short walks that Isabella noticed how many beggars would congregate outside the church and plead for pennies after the service was over. Miss Strawn never gave them a second glance, but it almost seemed like a purposeful reminder to all the girls of what would happen if they didn't hone their skills.

After church, the rest of the day was spent in the outdoor area or in the bed hall alongside mealtimes. It was the day they were most free, but also the day that got the most punishments for uncleanliness. Isabella and Nancy always made sure to check each other periodically throughout the day to escape the sting of Miss Strawn's cane.

Isabella knew she wouldn't have survived long without Nancy, but with her help, she found that a year passed by without too much suffering. The sting of the loss of her parents was still there, but it had begun to soothe with both time and Nancy's company.

She had done her best to keep track mentally of how much time was passing, but it became easier once Nancy stole a piece of paper from morning lessons which Isabella could then use to keep tally.

It was on the three hundred and thirty-sixth day of her stay at the orphanage, that a stranger arrived which would yet again change Isabella's life. Because on that day, her aunt turned up.

CHAPTER 5

Just as the previous fateful day had begun, this three hundred and thirty-sixth day began like any other. Isabella and Nancy slogged their way through morning lessons, made sure to carefully clean up after lunch, and Isabella even decided to tell one of her classic stories: "The Zebra Who Learnt to Fly". She had found she soon ran out of stories to tell about her own life, and started to come up with purely fictitious ones. The other girls didn't seem to mind, some even enjoyed the fantastical tales more. They allowed for an escape from their monotonous existence. Little did Isabella know, her escape was coming in the form of Margaret Bloom.

Isabella sat watching Nancy attempt to get what seemed like a wine-stain out of an old and faded yellow blouse, when Miss Strawn entered the room and called loudly, "Isabella, please come into my office. You have a visitor." All eyes swivelled to stare at Isabella. The words didn't register at first, and she couldn't move.

"Isabella." Miss Strawn's voice had a tension in it that Isabella had never heard before. "Do not make me tell you again." This quickly made Isabella's muscles move, almost by instinct. When Miss Strawn made a demand, you did the best you could to carry it out.

The walk across the classroom felt like the longest Isabella had ever taken. She knew everyone was staring at her. No one ever had visitors. Ever.

A quick glance to Nancy showed that even she was looking on in surprise and curiosity.

Isabella took a deep breath as she reached Miss Strawn. "Yes, Miss?"

"Follow me." Miss Strawn turned and walked briskly out. Isabella had to walk at double time to keep up with her. They strode in silence to Miss Strawn's office - a room Isabella had never seen the inside of - and Miss Strawn opened the door.

Inside was as efficiently bare and cold as Isabella expected. There was a large desk, a window on the far side of the room, and a large chair to match the desk. A slightly smaller chair sat on the other side of the desk, and in it sat... Isabella's mother?

Isabella rubbed her eyes in surprise. Surely they were just playing tricks on her. On closer inspection, it became clear that the lady was not in fact her mother, but had such a striking resemblance to her that it couldn't be a coincidence. The only thing that gave her away were eyes. Her mother's were a hazel brown, whereas this lady's were a sea green.

The lady who looked like her mother stood up when she saw Isabella. Her face breaking out in a wide smile.

"Isabella, say hello to Miss Margaret Bloom." Miss Strawn walked around to sit on her large chair behind the large desk.

"Hello Miss Margaret Bloom." Isabella said cautiously, as she took a small step into the office.

"Oh please," The lady stepped forward and knelt down to Isabella's level. "Call me Aunt Maggie."

Aunt Maggie. Aunt?

Isabella looked from Miss Margaret Bloom - Aunt Maggie - to Miss Strawn in confusion. What did this mean?

"I'm you mother's sister, little one." Aunt Maggie said softly. "I only ever got to see you once, when you were very small. You probably don't remember me at all."

"You look just like mummy." That was all Isabella could manage to say.

Aunt Maggie's smile seemed to get even bigger. "Yes, people said that to us all the time. Though people seemed to always like her eyes more. Those pretty hazel things."

"Your eyes are very pretty too."

"Yes yes." Miss Strawn had put on a small pair of spectacles, and was examining various sheets of paper that she had spread out on the desk. "This is all very touching, but Miss Bloom, if you could be so kind as to talk out the details with me."

"Of course." Aunt Maggie gave Isabella a quick affectionate pat on the head, and then returned to sit opposite Miss Strawn. "I'm Isabella's aunt, and I would like custody of my niece."

"And how has it come about that you've suddenly turned up out of the blue?" Miss Strawn said. "I was informed that all avenues of possible guardians were explored before Isabella was delivered to me. Did you turn her down a year ago?"

"I didn't know about anything that had happened." Aunt Maggie replied quick as fire. "If I had been informed, I would have gladly brought my niece in under my roof. It seems the avenues were not as well explored as you have been brought to believe."

Miss Strawn studied Aunt Maggie from above her spectacles. "And how does one's sister and brother-in-law get murdered, and their niece left with no one, without one's knowing about it?"

A determination set in Aunt Maggie's face. Isabella recognised it from her own mother's face. Isabella could already tell that the two were so alike in some ways, and completely different in others.

"Well, Miss Strawn, when one finds themselves with dead

parents and no other living family, as many if not all these girls here could relate to, and living in Liverpool instead of London, news travels quite slow." Aunt Maggie didn't let Miss Strawn interrupt and continued. "And when as you put it, all avenues are explored, that must not include the avenue leading to the road that leads to Liverpool, because I was never informed of what happened to my sister or her child my niece." She glanced at Isabella apologetically. "And to explain my sudden appearance, I've recently moved back to London, and was familiarising myself with the streets, when I came across the names of two people I loved dearly, Oscar and Lucy Farmerson, that's my sister and her husband, just making sure you're keeping up. I came across their names—" Aunt Maggie caught here for breath, and also to quench the lump that was forming in her throat. "I came across their name, Miss Strawn, chiseled into two gravestones. And I'm sure you must agree, that would come as quite a surprise to one's self."

"It would, Miss Bloom. But—"

"But then I realised," Aunt Maggie jumped off of Miss Strawn's last word. "That my sister had a daughter, and she didn't have a gravestone, so she must still be out there. That is a rather fair assumption to make, isn't it?"

"It is. Though I might—"

"So I decided to ask around, find out what I could about the beautiful couple that were tragically taken from this world too soon in such an unnatural way." Again, Aunt Maggie flashed an apologetic glance at Isabella. She was being very candid, but only because she knew it was the only way to convince this Miss Strawn to give up Isabella. "And I especially asked about their daughter, the one without a gravestone. And that led me here, to your establishment and to my niece." Aunt Maggie rapped her knuckles on Miss Strawn's desk. "So if that clears up everything fine and dandy, please draft up the necessary paperwork and I'll get out of your hair, your hat, and your way."

Isabella had never seen Miss Strawn speechless before, but somehow, her incredible Aunt had rendered her so. Miss Strawn's mouth opened and closed and finally opened again as she said. "This is highly irregular Miss Bloom, and I must say—"

"Adoptions are highly irregular at an adoption centre." Aunt Maggie's voice dripped with a wryness, and Isabella had to hold in her giggle. "That seems a little alarming to me, Miss Strawn. Doesn't it to you?"

"We're an orphanage, Miss Bloom, not an adoption centre."

"And I'm a lady not a woman. I fail to see how that distinction makes any difference in me walking out of here with my niece. Because, as you can probably tell – I've been told that it is very clear even after only moments of meeting me— that I am a rather persistent lady. You know that story in the Bible about the nagging housewife, they based that one on me." Aunt Maggie let out a chuckle at her own quip. "So please Miss Strawn, save both you, me, and this wonderful little girl sitting in this office all afternoon, and write up the papers." Aunt Maggie paused for a moment, for maximum effect. "Thank you kindly for the gracious and generous work you're doing for all these little girls."

Miss Strawn took in a deep laboured breath, and Isabella realised she had been holding her own. Her heart yearned to leave with Aunt Maggie, finally, to be a part of a home and family again. But in that excitement, a fear also niggled inside; her world would change yet again, and what would happen to Nancy?

Miss Strawn reached down into a draw in her desk, and without a word, pulled out a few sheets of paper. She pushed her spectacles up her face, again without a word, and gave Aunt Maggie a hard stern scowl.

The two woman sat staring down each other in silence for what seemed like an eternity to Isabella, but couldn't have been more than ten seconds. Isabella was sure that if a pin dropped, it would have sounded like an explosion.

"What's your current place of residence, Miss Bloom?" It seemed Miss Strawn was doing her best to not grind her teeth. "For the... necessary paperwork."

Aunt Maggie smiled and winked at Isabella. It was decided, Isabella was going home with her.

CHAPTER 6

"She did what?" Nancy gasped, as did the other girls near enough to overhear their conversation.

"My Aunt left Miss Strawn speechless. Put her in her place." Isabella said.

"Well then," Nancy scoffed. "About time someone did that I'd say." There were some murmurs of agreement. "So does that mean you're getting out of here?"

Isabella nodded. "They are just finishing up the paperwork. I leave with her today. Just need to pack my things… And say my goodbyes."

The word goodbye hung in the air. Neither girl really knew how to go about it. They had been a part of each other's lives every day for an entire year now. A year of them against the world, their story being forged, but now…

"I am so so happy for you." Nancy said as tears started to fall from her eyes, and she pulled Isabella into a hug. "Besides, the story would get pretty stale if it just stayed in this stuffy orphanage forever." Nancy did her best to laugh at her joke, and Isabella tried her best too. They stayed in the hug.

"I promise I'll come back for you." Isabella said. "It is *our* story after all."

They finally pulled out of the hug, but it was difficult. It felt like ripping a limb off. Nancy wiped the tears that kept falling, and shook her head, doing her best to talk through the oncoming sobs. "Yeah, 'The Solo Adventures of Isabella' just doesn't have the same ring to it as 'Izzy and Nancy Extraordinaire' does it?"

"Not at all." Isabella was sobbing now too. "We definitely should make sure that second option is the final name of the book."

"Oh it's a book now is it?" Nancy said.

"It is." Isabella said. "It's going to be a book with a green cover and gold trimmings."

"Hm…" Nancy considered. "I demand silver trimmings. It's more classy."

Isabella finally laughed properly. "Silver trimmings then. To be classy."

"We are the classiest after all." Nancy laughed too. The moment settled. "Goodbye for now, Izzy. I truly hope life with your Aunt is as wonderful as you deserve."

"I won't say goodbye. I'll just say… See you later." Isabella smiled.

Miss Strawn stepped into the room, with Aunt Maggie close behind her. "It's time, Isabella. I hope you have all your things packed. We don't want to keep Miss Bloom waiting." The sarcasm in her voice was evident, but the sentiment was true for Isabella.

Her life was changing yet again, but this time, hopefully for the better.

CHAPTER 7

The journey home had been lovely. They had walked, but Aunt Maggie had asked Isabella all about her life and what she had been up to the past year. She didn't speak down to Isabella in anyway, she was having a conversation with a person, not just a child. Isabella regaled her with the tale of how she had to say goodbye to Mrs Paxton, and then how Nancy had been her saviour at the orphanage, and even how she was the resident story spinner at the place. Aunt Maggie seemed to be almost proud of Isabella for that fact. "And now I've said goodbye to Nancy, and…"

"And hello to your Aunt Maggie." Aunt Maggie did her best to comfort Isabella. "I'm not going to disappear from your life, not now that I've finally found you." Isabella had looked deep into the green of her Aunt's eyes. Aunt Maggie's house was small but cozy. The district was "kind of sketchy if you don't have your eyes open" as Aunt Maggie put it, but relatively safe. Her house had a blue door with slightly chipped paint. When they got inside, Isabella was hit by how familiar it smelt to her old home, but with an unrecogniseable difference. The nostalgia of it all made Isabella a bit teary all over again. She couldn't detect any agenda or lie in them.

Aunt Maggie also told Isabella a bit of her life story too. She spoke of how she and Lucy hadn't always gotten along as children – "I was too adventurous and reckless for her I think." but had loved each other. When Lucy had married Oscar, Maggie had lived with her parents until they both passed, and moved to Liverpool, just for a change of scenery. She'd never meant to fall out of touch with her sister, but it had just happened. Isabella could hear the regret in her Aunt's voice. But now she was back in London, having found an opportunity as a cleaner, and to be "the cool Aunt" as she had put it.

"I don't have a proper bedroom for you yet." Aunt Maggie apologised. "I didn't know I would be having another head under this roof when I bought the place. But I'm sure we can remake this room into a perfect little haven for you." Aunt Maggie showed Isabella a room which appeared to be used for storage at the moment. "Until then though," Aunt Maggie led her through to what must be the main bedroom. "You'll have to put up with my snoring until we can get you a bed." Aunt Maggie smiled that slightly mischievous grin that Isabella was already starting to recognise. "I'm just kidding, I don't snore. Too loudly. Do you snore Izzy?"

Isabella giggled.

THE STORAGE ROOM flourished in a wonderfully comfy bedroom for Isabella, and Aunt Maggie let her decorate it however she wanted. She even seemed to encourage her niece to express herself in the way she set out her room: there wasn't the restrictions of properness here.

The two became a dream team in no time. Aunt Maggie was

much more warm and caring than Miss Strawn ever was. She made sure to keep up Isabella's learning, ensuring she wouldn't fall behind or rusty in regards to her reading and writing skills. The way most days went was: the two would wake up at the crack of dawn to have a modest breakfast, Aunt Maggie would work through an English workbook that she had procured for Isabella, and they worked for an hour, and then the two would head off to work. Aunt Maggie cleaned a variety of different houses - ones similar to the house that Isabella had grown up in. She brought Isabella along with her, but never required her to work, though Isabella found herself wanting to most days. She learnt academic skills from their time studying in the mornings, and then she learnt practical housework skills as they worked throughout the day. In the evenings, Aunt Maggie would teach Isabella how to cook, and then after dinner, just as the moon was starting to rise over the building tops, it was Isabella's favourite time: story time.

Every night, Aunt Maggie would spin new tales about all sorts of things. Sometimes, it was stories set on the very streets the two of them lived on, and others, stories set in far off lands filled with characters who had names Isabella had never heard before, who used words Isabella didn't even think were even real. On special occasions, the stories would interlink, and characters from one would show up in another, or the story would be a continuation of one she had told who knows how long ago. Isabella couldn't fathom how Aunt Maggie kept track of all of them in her head, but she never seemed to falter, even keeping track of all the different voices she would use.

Isabella would always be so entranced with each tale, sat with her arms hugged around her legs as she listened enrapt. All of the stories would end with the hero overcoming all their adversities, and being victorious and "living happily ever after". Isabella liked that. She liked the comfort in knowing, no matter how dire some of the stories got, that good would prevail in the end.

"Do stories ever have sad endings, Aunt?" Isabella asked one night. "Or is that just in real life."

Aunt Maggie considered her answer carefully before replying. "Not all made up stories end happy, no, but I would say the best ones always do. At least in a sense of happiness, though it might not be found where the characters initially thought it would." There was a small pause before she continued. "And in the same ilk, not every real life story ends sadly either. There is always a chance to find joy, no matter how dark things may get. Like you, you're my joy and light in this world, my little Izzy." Her Aunt gave her a kiss on the forehead, and tucked her into bed. "I love you."

"I love you too." Isabella looked up into the face that she had known since she was born - only the eyes were different. The love had never been stronger though. She closed her eyes, and drifted off into dreams of the Snargoulpow from Florp-End meeting Fred the Postman from just down the street, and the two of them solved the mystery of who was stealing all the magpie's food from the park's bird feeder. Isabella dreamt with a smile on her face.

CHAPTER 8

Three years went by in a blur for Isabella, and now at fourteen, she was an integral part of Aunt Maggie's cleaning operation. The two of them had built up a comfortable list of clientele which kept them busy and paid. Isabella's cleanliness was honed to perfection due to her time under Miss Strawn's strict rules, which made her a very effective "work partner" as Aunt Maggie put it - "I could call you an apprentice, but if you ever did a job better than me, it would just be embarrassing wouldn't it? And I'm expecting you to exceed me at some point Izzy, so I'll just promote you to partner from the start." Aunt Maggie was always pragmatic, which was a fun juxtaposition to all the idealism she peppered throughout the stories she told.

Aunt Maggie was also incredibly business wise, able to negotiate fair payment and contracts. Isabella had known Aunt Maggie was good with words from her first interaction with Miss Strawn, but she also came to realise how well Aunt Maggie could read people too. She always seemed to know what mood people were in, as well as the right things to either cheer them up - in the case of Isabella herself - or give her a better deal when it came to the people she worked for. The thought struck Isabella once that perhaps her Aunt's characters all felt so real and deep because she was able to draw from the observations she had made in her day-to-day life. Even with the most fantastical tales, she always made sure to bring that bit of humanity. Even though she was only fourteen, Isabella was very perceptive, and could see that this understanding of humanity also brought such an empathy to her Aunt, and Isabella strived to have the same insight and empathy.

It got to a point with the stories, that only one an evening wasn't enough for Isabella, and Aunt Maggie found she couldn't quench the thirst her niece had for tales, but being the fast thinking woman that she was, she found a solution almost instantly. Many of their clients read both newspapers and magazines, which after they had been read, would be thrown away: thrown away by the cleaners. Maggie didn't feel guilty in snatching them up instead of placing them in the waste - and Isabella certainly appreciated it. With these, she had a seemingly never-ending fountain of writings to enthrall herself in. She liked the fact that the newspapers kept her updated with the current times, but her true love was still in the world of make believe, and the literary magazines with their wondrous variety of stories. Mirroring Aunt Maggie's, some were episodic and ongoing, and other's stood alone. As Isabella wasn't a conventional subscriber to these magazines, sometimes she would have to start a story at the second or third part, but she didn't mind — it meant she could use her imagination to come up with what had come before.

Isabella was always on the lookout for discarded newspapers and magazines when she worked now, and Aunt Maggie sometimes would catch her already glance through whilst still on the job. A quick tut from her Aunt though, and she would have the paper folded up and tucked away for later, getting back to work, but her mind would still be processing whatever she had managed to read.

One day though, the headline that she glanced at as she picked up the newspaper was too shocking to just tuck away for later. In fact, she stood with it in her hands and her mouth open for what felt like forever.

It read:

'SERIAL KILLER CAUGHT
CULPRIT OF THE FARMERSON CASE BROUGHT TO JUSTICE,
FOUR YEARS ON'

"Lost in your daydreams again, Izzy?" Aunt Maggie said, waving a duster in front of Isabella's nose to catch her attention again. Isabella didn't even flinch, her eyes were still locked on the headline.

Aunt Maggie looked down at the paper. Her smile dropped as soon as she read it over. "Oh..."

"I..." Isabella felt the words catch in her throat. It felt as if someone was strangling her, whilst drowning her at the same time. While at the orphanage, how many times had she had nightmares about this man? How many times had she tried to tell herself that if she ever found him, she would bring justice like in the stories? But now, he was caught, and though that meant that chapter of her life could finally close, it came without any of the necessary catharsis for emotional release.

Aunt Maggie gently took the paper out of Isabella's hands, and put it aside. She pulled her niece into a hug, and stroked her hair. "It's okay, my little chuck. It's going to be okay. How are we feeling?"

Isabella was honest. "I don't really feel anything."

"I understand. That's shock. Would you like to stay here whilst I finish, and then we can go home together? Or would you like to just go home?"

"No no." Isabella shook her head, and slowly leaned out of the embrace to look her Aunt in the eye. "I'll be okay. This is our last house for the day anyways. I can finish up."

"You sure?" There was no judgement in Aunt Maggie's voice.

"I'm sure. It'll..." Isabella sniffed. "It'll be good to have something to do right now. And... I don't want to be alone."

Aunt Maggie caressed Isabella's face. "You truly are amazing. You know that?"

Isabella didn't know how to reply, so she simply said: "I'll get to work on the streaks of mud at the backdoor I think." She took a step towards the exit to the room, before pausing to ask delicately, "Can you make sure to keep the newspaper. Later, I want to read the whole article. Later."

"Of course." Aunt Maggie gave a solemn nod. Isabella turned to exit, but was halted by Aunt Maggie's next words. "I love you."

"I love you too." Isabella gave a weak smile, and then went to tend to the mud streaks. She did her best to think only about the streaks of mud on the floor, and how with a scrub of a brush, she could gradually make them go away. Part of her wished she could scrub the world clean of monsters like the man who had taken her parents away from her. She caught the thought and threw it out. *Only think of the mud streaks for now. Those other thoughts can come later.*

Later.

CHAPTER 9

*L*ater came, and everything came crashing down on Isabella. She was able to simply hold onto the thought of mud streaks until they reached home. Aunt Maggie had stayed very quiet too; Isabella was sure she was also processing the news.

"Can I read the paper now?" Isabella had finally asked, after the two of them had gotten inside and taken off their shoes and coats.

"You don't have to do it straight away. Not if you don't want to."

"I want to." Isabella was certain, and her Aunt handed her the crumpled paper. Isabella found herself sitting on the floor itself as she read, she wanted to feel at least some sense of being grounded.

'SERIAL KILLER CAUGHT
CULPRIT OF THE FARMERSON CASE BROUGHT TO JUSTICE,
FOUR YEARS ON

. . .

Illustrious Serial Felon Henry Sloan has finally be taken into custody, and confessed to a multitude of crimes. These include both the robbery at the Carron's estate last year, the blackmail of a multitude of victims, and his confessions trailed all the way back even to the tragic murder of Oscar and Lucy Farmerson all those years ago. His face is grim, he knows what he's done, but one can't say if it has the trappings of remorse on it. The police have said...'

Isabella didn't manage to read anymore, as the tears had become too overwhelming. She could hear the sound of them hitting the paper: the quiet dull thuds, like explosion. She let the paper drop from her hands, so she could bring them up to her face. A guttural sound came from her, a sound she wasn't even aware she could make.

The monster of her nightmares had a name now. Henry Sloan. Henry Sloan was the man that killed her parents. Nothing had really changed, this information didn't kill her parents all over again, but it did bring everything back up to the surface. It was as if someone had callously thrown salt all over an open wound that could never truly heal. Isabella wept and wept, crying out.

"I'm here." That was her Aunt. She had crouched down and taken Isabella into her arms again, as she had done earlier that day when they had first read the headline. "I'm here my darling." Isabella could hear that Maggie was crying to, a sob in the timbre of a voice. "It's okay. It's okay. Just let it all out. We're safe here. It's just you and me."

The two of them sat on the floor, letting the flood of emotions wash over them. Aunt Maggie held onto Isabella, and

Isabella pressed herself into her Aunt for support. She could feel how soaked Maggie's shirt now was from Isabella's tears.

"I guess." Isabella finally managed to say as her sobs subsided. "I guess it is like in the stories this time. Justice prevailed eventually... Too late... It doesn't feel like it does when the good guys win in the stories though."

"No." Aunt Maggie's voice was very gentle, barely a whisper. "In a story, the teller constructs the tale to be the most emotionally satisfying, even if sometimes it stretches the reality of things sometimes. We want the story to end happily, but even more so, we want the story to satisfy us.

And real life isn't always so kindly satisfying..."

"I wish I could just climb into one of your stories and live there. Everything is more simple at Florp-End."

Aunt Maggie laughed. "Yes it is, with the Snargoulpow. That's an old one..." The two sat in silence for a moment. "But if you did, then you would be leaving me behind!"

"You could come with me!" Isabella insisted.

"Now that is a nice thought." Aunt Maggie smiled, but her eyes were heavy. "In this world, in the tale that is our lives, we must never lose sight of the next chapter. Things are always darkest before the dawn. Who knows what the next page will hold for us both. This here..." Aunt Maggie motioned to the now discarded paper. "This is a very painful, frustrating, and down right unfair ending to one chapter, but let us see it as a chance to turn the page, and write the heading of the next."

"Chapter fifteen."

"Why chapter fifteen?"

"Well, I'm fifteen soon, so it just seems to make sense that each year is a chapter." Isabella pondered.

"I guess so. Though if we're going off my chapters." Aunt Maggie winked. "Well we don't need to get into how old I'm getting, do we?"

"You're not old!" Isabella cried out. "You're incredible."

"I could say the very same to you, little lady." Aunt Maggie stroked Isabella's forehead. "We share the book that is our life with many people, and I am so so happy that I get to share the rest of my chapters with you."

Isabella thought of all the people she had already shared her life book with. Mrs Paxton. Nancy. Aunt Maggie. She even shared it with Henry Sloan, though he would become only a footnote eventually. Eventually.

"Can we go to their graves?" Isabella asked. "Just... It feels right to, I'm not sure. Tell them he was caught, or something..."

Aunt Maggie agreed. The two of them made dinner, a flavour-filled Mulligatawny Soup — Isabella's favourite dish — and then headed out to pay their respects to Oscar and Lucy.

Isabella made sure to leave a tulip at her mother's grave, as they were her favourites.

It was now time for Isabella to close the page of Chapter Fourteen, and open it to Chapter Fifteen.

CHAPTER 10

*A*unt Maggie let Isabella sleep in the morning after — she figured that the preposition and conjunction work could wait at least a day. She still found she needed to come into Isabella's room and gently wake her when it was time for breakfast.

"Up we get, chuck. We can't be late for work."

Isabella groaned in reply, pulling herself up to a seated position. The large bags under her eyes were very pronounced.

"Did you sleep?"

"Not much." Isabella croaked. "It was difficult to. But I'm up. I'm up!" Isabella pulled herself out the warm confines of her bed, and dragged herself to wash up before breakfast. She didn't notice the few scrap sheets of paper than fell off her covers and to the floor as she did so, but Aunt Maggie did. She picked them up, and looked over the prose clearly scrawled in Isabella's handwriting.

"What's this?" She asked at the breakfast table, holding up the papers.

"Oh it's nothing."

"Doesn't seem like nothing." Aunt Maggie pointed at the title as she read it. "Marvellous Maggie and her Sidekick Amazing Izzy in... The Stolen Jewel of Kingston." Aunt Maggie looked at Isabella with a twinkle in her eye. "It's got a nice ring to it. Did you write this?"

Isabella nodded. "I couldn't sleep, so I started to come up with a story to try and get me to drift off and... I like it so much that I decided to write some of it." Isabella tried to reach across and grab the sheets, but Aunt Maggie stopped her. "It's all rubbish probably."

"Don't sell yourself short. What's it about?"

"You can read it..." Isabella said slightly moody.

"I want to hear it from the storyteller's mouth though." Aunt Maggie said with a tinge of mischief in her voice. Again, she knew exactly what she needed to do to bring Isabella out of her shell, and out of her mood.

"Well..." Isabella began. "Marvellous Maggie is a detective, and she solves crimes, captures bad guys, saves people, and brings justice to her city."

"And where does she live? Where's *her* city?"

"Um..." Isabella hadn't thought of all the details yet. "Birmingham."

Aunt Maggie gasped in delight. "Wonderful! Birmingham! Go on, go on."

"At first, she solved all the crimes herself, but then one day-" Isabella pointed at the sheets of paper. "That's the day this story is about. One day the case was too tricky for Marvellous Maggie to solve on her own." A small gasp of excitement from her Aunt spurred her on. "So she has to get the help of her niece, Amazing Izzy! And together they get to work on the case of the decade, maybe even the century! For the Jewel of Kingston has been lost!" Isabella raised her hands in showmanship. She quickly realised a rather poignant plot hole that had arisen from her decision of Birmingham. "This story is also set in London, Marvellous Maggie is on holiday there with

Amazing Izzy, so..." Isabella nodded, satisfied with her solution to the problem.

"And does the dynamic duo catch the crook and retrieve the jewel?" Aunt Maggie asked.

"I don't know. I haven't finished it yet." Isabella let some of her porridge fall off her spoon as she pondered. "I'm sure they will though. Marvellous Maggie is marvellous after all."

"And let's not forget that Amazing Izzy is amazing!" Aunt Maggie tickled Isabella, and she giggled. "You should continue writing it."

"No no." Isabella shook her head. "It was just a silly thing... A game to help me pass the time."

"But I'd like to read the rest of it!" Aunt Maggie insisted. "I want to know who stole the jewel and how they get it back! You can't leave me hanging in suspense now, can you?"

"I guess not..." Isabella smiled.

"Tell you what." Aunt Maggie got up to start clearing the table. "How about we switch between your work books, and you writing more of your tales each morning? I'm sure putting what you learn into practise will hone your skills even more. How does that sound to you?"

That sounded like an incredible idea to Isabella. A scary one too though — she had never really put any of her stories down on paper. That made them permanent, that made them a thing that could be judged. She knew though that Aunt Maggie would be a very gracious critic, and help her excel even more.

CHAPTER 11

*I*sabella did end up finishing 'Marvellous Maggie and her Sidekick Amazing Izzy in The Stolen Jewel of Kingston' over the next week. Sometimes she found it difficult to get the story down how she wanted on the page, and other times it would simply flow as easily as water down a river. She felt so proud when she could finally hand the finished story to her Aunt to read through.

Aunt Maggie loved the story, and asked for another heart pulsing drama starring the detective duo, and Isabella got to work on her next story. Once that story was done, she wrote another, and another, and another.

She started branching out into other genres starring other characters, but Aunt Maggie's favourites were always the Marvellous Maggie and Amazing Izzy tales.

By seventeen, Isabella had accumulated an impressive literary canon, which Aunt Maggie stored in a special cupboard in the house — both of their most treasured place.

Isabella also continued to collect and read the newspapers and literary magazines. She stumbled across a magazine one day called *'Bentley's Miscellany'* which had the first part of the story that would come to be her favourite: *'Oliver Twist'*. She had saved reading that one until she was at home and all settled so she could properly focus on it.

It was wordy, very wordy, probably the wordiest thing she had ever read up until this point. This was clear even from the first chapter which was titled:

'TREATS OF THE PLACE WHERE OLIVER TWIST WAS BORN AND OF THE CIRCUMSTANCES ATTENDING HIS BIRTH'

SOMETIMES ISABELLA WOULD HAVE to reread a sentence or passage to truly understand the meaning, but she didn't mind. It meant she could spend more time in this world with the illustrious characters that the writer — Charles Dickens — had invented. She loved the titular Oliver, and how he faced the cruelty of the world, even though he didn't have any parents. In many ways, she saw herself in Oliver, especially when he was in the awful orphanage, though she knew she was so blessed and lucky to now be living with Aunt Maggie who lauded her talents and passion, instead of trying to crush and conform her into a box.

It was tricky to keep up with the story, as it came out in monthly instalments in the magazine, so Isabella had to do her best to make sure to keep on the lookout for each issue. A certain household became her haven, as it always seemed to have the latest instalment of 'Bentley's Miscellany', and it always eventually ended up in the pile ready to be thrown away. Isabella always got excited and nervous whenever they went to clean there. *What if the next instalment has already come and gone and I've missed it?*

Over the three years that the story was released, Isabella

manage to not miss a single instalment. It was sometimes close calls. On one occasion, she had to chase down another maid who was taking all the papers out, but she had done it!

She now stood in the hallway of the Pennington's reading the final instalment of the saga. She knew she should have saved it for later when she was home, but she couldn't help herself.

'THE FORTUNES *of those who have figured in this tale are nearly closed. The little that remains to their historian to relate, is told in few and simple words.'*

ALL SHE HAD LEFT WAS this epilogue, that explained what had happened to the remaining characters, where and who they had ended up with. She couldn't believe that after so long, she was finally reaching the end of all of these people stories, at least in regards to the story being written by Mr Dickens. She was sure the characters would all stay with her for the rest of her life, and in the little hours of the morning, when dreams and day dreams mix, she would forge her own ideas of where they ended up next and what they got up to. She wouldn't be able to help herself.

Isabella whispered the final words as she read them. "I believe that the shade of Agnes sometimes hovers round that solemn nook. I believe it none the less because that nook is in a Church, and she was weak and erring..." And just like that, it was finished. A small tear trickled down and splatted on the magazine next to the those final lines of prose.

"A cleaner reading? Now that's a sight you don't see everyday." A unfamiliar voice snapped Isabella out of her trance, and she had to hold in a yelp of surprise as she spun around, instinctively hiding the magazine behind her back in embarrassment and shame. Isabella didn't recognise the person who had spoken. He was a young man, perhaps in his mid-twenties, with hazelnut coloured eyes, and mouse brown hair. He was looking at her with bemusement. "Not an unwelcome sight though. No need to be ashamed, or hide... What are you reading there?" He motioned to the magazine that was clearly in her hand even though it was behind her back.

She sheepishly brought it around for him to see, showing off the cover. "It's Bentley's Miscellany, sir. It was the final part of a story I've been following for years, and I just got caught up, and I know I shouldn't get distracted whilst working, but you know, after three years of—"

The young man cut her off politely. "It's okay. Like I said, you don't need to be ashamed. I'm not going to tell you off for getting invested in a good story, I do the same myself. And three years did you say? Three years of waiting to know how a story ends? I wouldn't be able to wait until the day was almost over, not when it was right there in my hand." The young man took a step towards Isabella, and held out his hand for the magazine. "May I?"

"Of course, sir." Isabella dutifully handed him the magazine. Secretly she hoped he wouldn't keep it, as she was planning to take it home to be able to reread it again.

"Don't worry about calling me sir or anything." The young man smiled. He had a very nice smile. "Oh wait! Of course, I haven't introduced myself or anything. Or even asked your name! I'm so sorry. I get caught up when it comes to stories and writing. Tutor, you see?" The young man held out his hand to shake Isabella's. "My name is Oliver Guildman. And yours?"

Isabella's mouth dropped open. She had never been treated like this before in one of these posh houses. Her employers had always been polite enough, but never truly invested in their conversations with her. She was there for a function, and as long as she fulfilled the function well, they would all get along. But this young man... Oliver. He was standing there smiling with his hand outstretched for a handshake having asked her name.

She realised she had been standing in silence with her mouth agape for who knows how long. She cleared her throat and hastily said. "I'm Izzy. I mean, Isabella. Isabella Farmerson. I'm the cleaner." She shook his hand. It was soft and warm. She also noticed how amazing he smelt. What was going on?

"Miss Farmerson. I've caught glimpses of you. You've been cleaning here for quite a while now?" Oliver didn't seem to just be making polite small talk. He seemed genuinely interested.

Isabella nodded. "About a year and a half now."

"You must do a good job. The Pennington's house always looks immaculate to me." Oliver smiled as he glanced down at the magazine. "Bentley's Miscellany… I've heard of this one. Richard Bentley I believe, he's the man who runs it. Only started relatively recently. I've heard mixed but interesting things about it. Which story in particular was ending?"

"Oliver Twist." Isabella smiled. She already felt comfortable with Oliver. "Quite ironic isn't it? Seeing as you have the same name."

"Irony too? I'm impressed." If someone else had said that, Isabella would have felt patronised, but for some reason she couldn't quite explained, it didn't feel like anything but a shining compliment coming from Mr Guildman. "If you don't mind me asking, how do you know about irony? Arthur's still getting to grasps with such rhetoric." Arthur was Mr Pennington's fourteen year old son, who must be the pupil Oliver tutored here.

"My Aunt teaches me." Isabella said. "We worked through workbooks every morning for the first couple years that I lived with her, and I read all I could find. Newspapers, literary magazines, and I…" She hesitated, but Oliver's kind eyes gave her the confidence to continue. "And I've been writing my own stories for quite a while now too. Just for my Aunt to read, no one else."

"Well I would certainly love to read one some time, Isabella." Oliver said. "I love finding new storytellers, hearing how they put words to the page, how they bring characters to life."

"I..." Isabella was once again speechless. Someone so above her station, someone with a real proper education, was interested in her stories? He was interested in her prose?

"I'm sorry." Oliver said into the silence. "I sometimes get too forward when it comes to writings and... I didn't mean anything improper by my request, and—"

"Oh no!" It was Isabella's turn to politely interrupt. "It wasn't that, just... No one but my Aunt has ever read one of my stories. It's just..."

"Exciting but terrifying all at the same time?"

"Yes!"

"I know the feeling." Oliver said. "Not well, I don't write much anymore, found my calling in teaching, but every so often I pen a little limerick or something. Nothing as illustrious as what you've done it seems."

Isabella could feel her cheeks getting warm as she blushed at the praise. "I can maybe bring one next time I'm here, what sort of stories do you like, sir- I mean, Mr Guildman?"

"Since you've already surprised me so much already, Miss Farmerson" Oliver smiled. "Surprise me. I'm sure whatever it is, it'll be an incredibly engaging read."

"Don't get your expectations to high." Isabella was already mentally sorting through the cupboard back home that contained all her manuscripts — which should she give to Mr Guildman? These stories were a part of her, such a personal thing, and for some inexplicable reason, she wanted to make sure she presented a proper but exciting part of her to him. He was giving her his attention and time, she wanted to prove she was worthy of it as a fellow academic, regardless of class or education.

Before she could say anything else, their conversation was

interrupted by yet another surprising voice — Mr Pennington's. "Miss Farmerson, can you come into my study for a moment? There's something I need to talk to you about." The door to his study had opened, and the imposing man was now stood in it looking out into the hallway at them.

There was a naturally imposing nature to Mr Pennington, he was a businessman with a lot of money. Isabella wasn't sure whether he had simply inherited it, or if he had scrapped and fought his way up the industrial ladder. She wouldn't be surprised if the latter was the case. He had an ability similar to Aunt Maggie's, an innate talent for reading people. Though his specialty was more what a he could give to a client, and more importantly what they could give to him. His hair was slightly thinning on the top, but only the sides had greyed so far, and it was purposefully styled. Isabella recognised the hairstyle, as she had seen his son Arthur with the same, though it seemed to sit on Mr Pennington better.

Isabella's blood ran cold and her heart felt like it skipped at least two beats. What could Mr Pennington need to talk to her about? All the possible worst case scenarios sped through her head before she could even get a word out. Finally she managed to say something. "Of course, Mr Pennington. Right away."

"How are you, Oliver? Arthur doing well?" Mr Pennington said.

"Yes, sir. I've started incorporating some Latin into our studies, just to try and keep him on his toes." There was a tinge of something in Oliver's reply that Isabella couldn't quite decipher. "Miss Farmerson, I'll let you go. Thank you for introducing me to Mr Twist who I share a name with, and I look forward to whatever you bring." Oliver handed Isabella back the magazine, his hands only slightly brushing hers as he did so, nodded at Mr Pennington, and took his leave.

Isabella turned to Mr Pennington. If he was wondering what business a lowly cleaner had talking with the tutor of his son, he didn't ask. He simply motioned for her to exit the hallway into his study, leaving the door open as he walked back into it. Isabella quickly and quietly slipped the literary magazine into her satchel, and followed him in.

Although her and Aunt Maggie cleaned all over the Pennington's house, his office was always off limits. Mr Pennington had always insisted on Arthur being the one to clean up any mess he made during his lessons, and Isabella guessed the same rules applied to himself in regards to his office. Aunt Maggie had applauded Mr Pennington privately to Isabella one night, for his "strong sense of character, and an attention to maintaining it in himself and building it up in his son."

Seeing the office for the first time felt very intimidating, especially under the unknown circumstances. On two sides of the room, bookcases were stacked high with all kinds of books. Most of them looked to be non-fiction, though Isabella did catch a glance at some that seemed — at least from the titles and spines — to be fiction. An impressive fireplace drew the attention of the eye, which would then naturally travel to the two arm chairs that sat facing it, and then to the imposing desk positioned just to the right.

Mr Pennington went and sat in one of the arm chairs, and motioned for Isabella to take a seat in the one opposite. "Please Miss Farmerson, feel free to sit." His mood and intention was still unreadable. Isabella took a seat, perched on the edge of the arm chair.

"Now." Mr Pennington began with a business-like tone. "How do you like it here, Miss Farmerson? Is the house manageable, the work desirably enough, as cleaning work goes?"

Was this a trick question of some kind? Was Mr Pennington trying to catch Isabella out for something she wasn't aware of? You can't always spot the trap if you don't know what to look for. Isabella decided to simply answer honestly. "I like working here very much, Mr Pennington. Your family is rather clean anyways."

"Yes." Mr Pennington nodded in thoughtful agreement. "Darcy, my late wife that is, Darcy always made sure me and Arthur stayed in line, cleaned up after ourselves." He smiled fondly, with an air of melancholy. "Even once we could afford maids and cleaners, she always liked to have a lot of the work done before they came."

Isabella didn't know how to respond. She had wondered where Mrs Pennington was, but she hadn't realise that Mr Pennington was a widower.

"She passed about seven years ago." Mr Pennington stated, before taking in a breath and clearing his throat. "My apologies Miss Farmerson, I didn't mean to get lost in thought."

"It's no trouble, Mr Pennington. I'm sorry for your loss."

"No need to be sorry. We all lose people, don't we?" Mr Pennington couldn't have realised how poignant of a question that was to Isabella, and quickly moved on. "But back to the present, and the business at hand. Your work here." She had almost forgotten that they were discussing her work, though for what reason she still couldn't deduce. "When Miss Bloom brought you in, I must admit at first I was slightly trepidations, but you proved all my worries wrong, and exceeded all my expectations."

The panicked worry that had been gradually taking over started to retreat, this certainly wasn't what Isabella had expected. "Thank you, sir."

"Miss Barnsley and I have been discussing bringing on someone full-time as another maid to aid Dawn. With Arthur only growing older, and my work only becoming more cumbersome, we both feel it would be prudent and necessary. And we both agreed that we would like to offer you the position."

A permanent job? She *definitely* was not expecting that.

"A full-time position here." Isabella wasn't sure whether

what she had just said was a statement or a question, but it had slipped out.

"Yes." Mr Pennington continued. "The pay would obviously be better, we look after our own and all that motto-nonsense. Though I do want you to know I don't think taking care of my own is nonsense, just how some businessmen commodify the notion of human decency." He chuckled to himself. "We would also be able to offer you lodgings here, as well as three meals a day in the servant quarters. I understand we would also be stealing you away from your Aunt, Miss Bloom, but you'll always be free to visit her on your days off."

Isabella hadn't considered that. For the past seven years, it had always been her and her Aunt: the dynamic duo. Even when Isabella got old enough to take cleaning jobs on by herself — as she had been doing with the Pennington's house for a while now — each night the two would converge and share stories from the day. If she took on this position, that wouldn't happen anymore. Her evenings would be bookended with the telling of a tale. The thought scared her.

"May I think on it, Mr Pennington?" Isabella said. "I am so grateful for you thinking of me, and for the offer. It's just, as you said, I've been with my Aunt for so many years now, I would like to be able to ask what she thinks. I wouldn't want to leave her out to dry, I'm sure you understand?" She hoped he did.

"Of course. I would expect nothing less from such a level-headed girl as yourself. Take some time to think about it, and get back to me. Shall we say, by the end of next week? Though if you make up your mind sooner, we can take you on when you are ready."

"Thank you, sir."

"For safety's sake." Mr Pennington had a shine of amusement in his eye. "To help my case, I can also promise that you shall have access to any literary magazine or newspaper that arrives also."

Isabella froze. She hadn't realised her interest in the papers had been noticed. "I'm sorry, sir. I always made sure that I only took papers that were going to be thrown away. I never stole anything, or if I have, I never meant to. If there is something that you need returning I can—"

Mr Pennington laughed. It was a kind laugh. "I am not accusing you, Miss Farmerson. I applaud someone who makes sure to keep themselves up to date with our goings on, as well as honing their vernacular. If you come on full-time, you shan't have to wait until the papers are being thrown away. In fact, if there's any particular magazines you would like, I can look into gaining subscriptions for them."

"Well you are already subscribed to my favourite, sir." Isabella was surprised how candidly she was already speaking. "Bentley's Miscellany."

"Ah yes." Mr Pennington said. "It seemed to catch the eye of Mr Guildman as well, didn't it?"

Her cheeks flushed again at the thought of Mr Oliver Guildman taking such an interest in her. "It did seem to do so, sir. He seems like a very fine tutor for your son."

"By all accounts he is a very fine tutor. And do you know why, Miss Farmerson?"

Isabella shook her head. She could think of a few reasons, but she wasn't sure if they were the type of reasons Mr Pennington would subscribe to also.

"Because he cares about what he's teaching. That's the sign of a great teacher and worker. If you can find someone that cares, that has passion and drive, you've found something very special." Mr Pennington pointed at Isabella. "I think I see that drive in you. Maybe not necessarily a passion for scrubbing floors, but for making sure you do the best job you can. Miss Barnsley agrees with me. That's why we're offering you this job Miss Farmerson. I do hope you decide to take us up on the offer."

"Full-time. Better pay. Three meals a day." Aunt Maggie listed all the information Isabella had thrown her way as soon as her niece had come rushing through the door. "It seems like an incredible offer to me Izzy. I think you should definitely take it."

"But what about you, Auntie?" Isabella said, pacing back and forth across the room as she thought. "If I accept, I go and live with them."

"They don't live too far away."

"It feels far."

"It's not Liverpool, is it?" Aunt Maggie's eyes shone with slight mischief with that comment.

Isabella couldn't help but smile. "No, it's not Liverpool. And I would be able to come and visit quite often I'm sure. And the extra pay would be very helpful for us both, means you would need to work less even without me. And—"

"And and and." Aunt Maggie interrupted. "We can keep walking round in circles with 'ands' but we don't need to, do we dear? It's an amazing offer, you'll take it, and all shall be well."

Isabella let out the breath she didn't realise she had been holding. "All shall be well." It was decided, she would take the offer and move into the Pennington household.

"Well…" Aunt Maggie said pseudo-dramatically. "Here's to an exciting new chapter!"

CHAPTER 12

*A*ssimilating into the Pennington household was a rather seamless affair. Isabella moved in four days after making her decision — Mr Pennington wasn't exaggerating when he said they would be able to take her on as soon as she would desire. Now that she was to be living there, Isabella was introduced to everyone in the household. Alongside meeting Mr Pennington's son Arthur, Isabella met the handful of other employees who worked in and around the house.

All of them were led by the ever acute Miss Barnsley. This was the woman Mr Pennington had been referring to in Isabella's conversation with him — this was the woman who had chosen her as their top candidate.

Miss Barnsley was never cruel, but was she was strict only in the sense that she expected everyone to do their best work at all times. The older lady seemed to have the respect of everyone, including Mr Pennington.

"Now I understand you've been a cleaner most of your life, dear?" She had asked when helping Isabella set up her room. "I'm not going to ask much of you that you haven't already done. But I like things done my way. Obviously you won't know my way yet, and I'm assuming our ways will line up most of the time, but if they don't, I will require you to learn to work it my way if the time comes. Understood?" She was curt, but not impolite. Efficient and honest. Isabella liked her. "With just the master and his son in the house at the moment, work isn't too difficult, but I believe that might change soon." Miss Barnsley didn't reveal anything more.

Isabella's room wasn't anything too special, but it was comfortable. The servant's quarters downstairs were also pleasant — and very well kept thanks to Miss Barnsley's regime. Many of the servants opted to spend their downtime in the communal space they shared, rather than cooped away in their rooms.

There were quite a few people on the payroll, but Isabella did her best to keep track of everyone's names. There was James, who was Mr Pennington's driver. Dawn was the other maid alongside Isabella, she was very helpful in getting Isabella up to speed as to their various jobs, and the specific things that might require extra time or attention. Carlos was the cook, who not only prepared all the food for the Pennington's and their guests, but also all the meals for the servants. Isabella didn't know how he managed it all, but he was always humming to himself in a complete state of relaxation whenever Isabella crossed paths with him. Mr Turner was the butler, and William was his under-butler. Isabella didn't interact too much with either of them.

And of course, there was Mr Oliver Guildman, who Isabella would catch glimpses of in the study room teaching Arthur a variety of different subjects. Isabella had given him a handful of her short stories the next time she saw him after moving in. He had been extremely grateful, and promised he would read them soon. She didn't want to step out of place in the day-to-day, so never spoke to him out of turn, but she couldn't help always glancing for a moment longer or too whenever he was around.

Mr Pennington's son Arthur barely acknowledge Isabella's entrance into the household. Isabella didn't mind too much. He was at that age where the mixture of naive confidence and pubescent insecurity would make him stand-offish as well as extremely frustrated, seemingly with himself. Isabella didn't take his attitude towards her personally.

After about three weeks of working at the Pennington's, Oliver approached Isabella one day. In his hand were the stories she had given him, as well as the latest issue of Bentley's Miscellany.

"The stories were very well put together, Miss Farmerson." Oliver said. "I greatly enjoyed reading them all. I hope this job doesn't take up too much of your time that you must stop writing, I believe that would be a great loss to the world."

Isabella's entire being seemed to hum with warmth at his kind words. The feeling had returned when she retold the story to her Aunt the next time she had gone to visit her — which as Pennington had promised, could be often and consistent.

"Mr Guildman is so kind, and clever." Isabella said.

"And handsome?" Aunt Maggie asked.

"What?" Isabella was caught completely off guard by the question. "I suppose he is rather fetching. He isn't unpleasant to look at. Why do you ask?"

Her Aunt hadn't given her a satisfying response, simply smiling at her with a knowing look. Isabella didn't try and get anything more out of Maggie, she knew she wouldn't be able to.

∽

SOMETHING THAT NATURALLY OCCURRED, but didn't surprise Isabella, is she found her place in the troupe as the resident storyteller at meal times. At first it started out with the small talk she had with Dawn developing naturally into her portraying various stories from her life with words, but as the days and weeks went on, Carlos would sometimes join them to hear whatever tale Isabella would recount. Once he'd heard about it, James would try and find excuses to stay for dinner and hear Isabella spin stories. At some point, Jacob also had started appearing more often. Isabella didn't mind the audience, in fact, she relished in it. Miss Barnsley had never joined them, but Isabella had spotted her standing around a corner overhearing one of her stories. As long as it wasn't getting her in trouble, she would continue.

Isabella always felt the most herself, and the most at home, when she was telling a story. That's what she was: a storyteller.

It was during one of these story times that what Miss Barnsley had been alluding to all the way back when Isabella moved in came to light.

"The master is getting married!" Miss Barnsley declared one evening in the servants quarters. Everyone was gathered around Isabella, even Mr Turner. They all turned to stare at Miss Barnsley, dumbfounded.

"He's wha'?" Carlos finally asked after a long pause.

"Married? Again?" Dawn asked.

"So he's finally decided on it then has he?" Mr Turner turned to William and chuckled.

"I knew it!" James exclaimed.

Isabella just raised her eyebrows in surprise. That would mean another new person in the house, though Mr Pennington's new wife would get a vastly different welcome she was sure.

"It's a very respectable lady named Miss Vanessa Moorly." Miss Barnsley explained once they had all quieted down.

"I drove the two of them around a lot." James interjected. "They were very sweet together."

"Yes, James, thank you." Miss Barnsley's tone asked everyone to remain quiet until she had finished explaining. Everyone allowed her to finish. "Now Miss Vanessa is a widow, so we will also be welcoming three new children to the family and house." She gave everyone a look, making sure they got the significance of more children: children were messy, more mess, more work. "They are Lola, who is seventeen, she shouldn't add too much to the workload, and the twins David and Paul, who are both five years old. They are adorable little cherubs, but also still five year old boys. I remember what little Arthur was like at that age, so I can imagine what chaos double trouble will cause." She chuckled. "But we run a tight ship, and we will be able to handle this. And I'm sure we are all very happy for Mr Pennington himself. Darcy will always be missed, but this house could use a mother again I'd say." They all murmured in agreement.

Miss Barnsley clapped her hands together. "Well, the wedding is in two weeks, so we have no time to waste in preparation! Let's get to work people!"

CHAPTER 13

The wedding came and went. All the employees of Mr Pennington were invited, and he even let Isabella bring Aunt Maggie along as a guest. The two of them had great fun being able to dress themselves up.

Miss Vanessa looked stunning as the bride, and Isabella truly did feel happy for Mr Pennington. She hadn't known the man long, but the overwhelming joy he was feeling was evident on his face.

Even Mr Guildman had attended the wedding. Aunt Maggie had commented that he was 'rather fetching' as Isabella had said. "Perhaps even more fetching in that suit." Isabella felt her cheeks go warm, and Aunt Maggie laughed kindly.

Vanessa Moorly became Vanessa Pennington, and her and her three children moved in. Miss Barnsley's initial assessments were unsurprisingly accurate: Lola was a very quiet and shy young woman, who kept mostly to herself, and barely left a trace of disorder anywhere she went in the house. The twin boys, however, were a different matter entirely.

They would run into the house from outside without remembering to remove their shoes or boots, no matter how wet or muddy it was outside, and they would constantly forget to put things away that they had grabbed, sometimes absent-mindedly, sometimes with purpose. Isabella could never find herself getting too frustrated with them though. The two of them were constantly playing make believe with each other, and many times the reasons for their callousness or clumsiness was because they were wrapped up in whatever world they had concocted. Isabella saw a lot of herself in the twins, and adored them.

Miss Vanessa herself was a kind woman, and very respectful to all of the staff. Isabella could sense some tension between her and Arthur — mainly from Arthur — but if it ever manifested, Isabella never witnessed it.

Isabella did have her own moment of tension with Arthur, and it came about during one of the boy's lessons with Oliver.

She was dusting the small table that was positioned next to the doorway into the study, which had been left open, when she had noticed a dirty plate with crumbs left on it and an empty glass sat on a set of drawers in the study room. Without thinking, she decided to go in and pick up the dirty dishes.

As she did, she overheard Arthur imploring to Oliver: "I don't know! I don't know how it should end!"

"Come now, Arthur, you've done so well. You've constructed a great mystery, a compelling one, you've selected the best candidate for the culprit, or should I say culprits — was a stroke of genius having more than one — as well as what I would believe to be the best structure. Now all that's left to do is..." Oliver trailed off, to allow Arthur to answer.

"I know I know! Find the best thing to give the detective the one-up on the killer! Crack the case wide open and all... I just can't think of anything."

"A big house, much like this one. Lot's of different options."

"None I can see."

"What about a maid that overhead the murderer plotting?"

Isabella had spoken before thinking. She quickly clasped a hand over her mouth.

The two who were sitting at the table in the middle of the room turned to face her. Oliver's eyebrows raised in delighted surprise. Arthur's drooped in suspicion.

"What was that, Miss Farmerson?" Oliver asked.

"I... Well... I just..." Isabella stammered in embarrassment.

"You're asking the maid?" Arthur asked incredulously.

"Now now, Arthur." Oliver reprimanded him. "A good writer looks for inspiration in anything and everyone. And I happen to know that Miss Farmerson here is very well read. Please, what was your suggestion?"

Isabella began talking even as she felt the panic rise in her chest. If Miss Barnsley found out she so rudely interrupted the master's son's lesson... She hoped Arthur would keep quiet about it. "Well... If it's in a big house, that means there's servants. And you mentioned their being multiple culprits, so they must have discussed their plans at some point surely. So what better thing to crack a case wide open, than someone that goes unnoticed by so many?" Isabella tried to not sound too snarky towards Arthur with that last comment. "What if a maid of the household heard them plotting, but had kept silent out of fear. The detective, showing he's an upright and just man, gives her the confidence to speak up and testify, and that's how the case is closed?"

Oliver raised his eyebrows and looked across at Arthur for his thoughts. Arthur didn't say anything, just frowned and looked down at the paper and pencil. Oliver looked backed over at Isabella and smiled. "I personally think that would be a really interesting way to finish the story. Don't you Arthur?"

Arthur just muttered under his breath.

The reality of what Isabella had just done settled in for her. She felt her throat clench in embarrassment and shame. "I'm so sorry. I didn't mean to interrupt and disrupt the... Uh... I'm sure you will think of a perfectly stellar ending to your mystery Arthur, sir." Isabella quickly left the room before she could hear a reply from either of them.

She rushed down into the kitchen to deposit the dirty dishes, and to hide herself away for a few moments. How could she be so callous? Everyone had their place in the household and their part to play — and Isabella's definitely wasn't to partake in the studies of Arthur. She reprimanded herself, and got on with the rest of her work. The damage was done she supposed, and all she could do now was hope that Arthur — or even worse Oliver — didn't report her to Mr Pennington.

CHAPTER 14

Although the immediate panic had passed by dinner time, Isabella still had a gnawing feeling in the back of her mind; she couldn't feel relaxed and comfortable. Dawn and James were disappointed when Isabella admitted to not feeling great, meaning she wouldn't have a story for them this evening.

"Oi, Carlos!" James called into the kitchen at the chef who was preparing their meal. "You got any gooduns?"

Carlos walked out, somehow carrying four plates of food — on what must have been steaming hot plates — with ease. He set them down at the table as he replied. "My stories are no good. All end the same way."

"You save the day?" Dawn asked dryly.

"Of course." Carlos laughed. "Do I not always save the day?"

"He's got a point there, Dawnie." James chuckled.

Dawn just rolled her eyes. Isabella was only half listening.

Miss Barnsley appeared at the doorway that led into the rest of the house and cleared her throat. "Is everything and everyone nice and proper?" Isabella knew she was mostly joking, but there was a tinge of seriousness to the question. They all looked to her. "We have a visitor."

She stepped aside to reveal Oliver, who sheepishly walked in. He gave an endearingly awkward wave.

"Hullo." James said. "Mr Guildman, right? Teacher."

"Tutor." Oliver replied, before quickly correcting himself. "But teacher also works. Either or." He took a second to collect himself before continuing. "I just came down to request an audience with Miss Farmerson?" Oliver looked over at Isabella, as did everyone else in the room.

Isabella could tell that James was holding in his laughter. Dawn just looked shocked. Carlos was unreadable. Miss Barnsley's expression was also perfectly serene, though Isabella could spot a small glimmer of amusement in her eyes.

Isabella cleared her throat. "Yes. What do you need Mr Guildman?"

Oliver took a step into the room. "It's not really a need, more so a question, or a series of them."

"Right. Well, I'm all yours."

Oliver glanced at the other's sitting around the room, and then to Miss Barnsley. She gave a performative sigh. "Alright, the rest of us, let's go eat in the kitchen, shall we? Give Isabella and the *tutor* privacy." As she passed by Isabella she whispered. "I'm just next door if anything unsavoury happens. Just give me a call."

"I'm sure it will be fine." In reality Isabella wasn't sure. Perhaps Mr Guildman had come down to scold and admonish her for earlier. No one ever likes being lectured, but Isabella found the thought of Mr Guildman in particular doing so even more unpleasant.

As soon as everyone else had shuffled off into the kitchen Isabella stood up and jumped into a flurry of apology. "Mr Guildman if this is about earlier, I want you to know that I am very aware of how improper and impolite my actions were. I never meant to impose or imply that your teaching—"

"Woah woah woah." Mr Guildman smiled. "This isn't about

earlier. Well, actually it is, but I'm not here in annoyance or to tell you your place. Also, feel free to simply call me Oliver. Mr Guildman is my father."

Isabella chuckled at Oliver's quip. "Alright, Oliver. Though I would request you call me Isabella in return."

"Well, Isabella." Oliver smiled at the usage of her first name. "I wanted to come down and compliment you on the skill you showed earlier. You came up with a very interesting concept almost instantaneously. Have you read much mystery fiction? Detective stories and the like?"

"A few pieces here and there." Isabella said. "My Aunt used to tell me stories with culprits and detectives. She always had a soft spot for those who chased justice."

"And was the maid being the key witness a part of any of those?"

Isabella shook her head. "I don't believe so."

"Isabella's dead good at coming up with things on the spot!" A voice piped up from the kitchen: it was James. Isabella could hear both Dawn and Miss Barnsley shush him.

Both Isabella and Oliver couldn't help smiling.

"You have a real talent, Isabella." Oliver took a step towards her. "A natural prowess for storytelling. I saw that from the stories you lent me, and from your quick thinking today. And I had the thought, as long as you were interested and wouldn't mind. What if we worked together some time? I can teach you some things, and I'm sure I'll learn plenty from you too. Think of it more like a mutual discussion and exploration, than a tutor and student."

"Oh, I don't have the money for any sort of tutorship Mr Guild- Oliver. Nor the time in the day to take lessons."

"I wasn't thinking of asking for payment at all!" Oliver said. "What I can learn from you would be payment enough in many ways. I appreciate that you are very busy, however, and I wouldn't want to burden you in any way."

"It wouldn't be a burden. I don't think you're capable of being a burden." Isabella had let out the compliment before thinking. She stammered, trying to recover. "My only real free time is now. Dinner time, that is."

"Let's work over dinner then." Oliver suggested. "I'll have plenty of time to finish up with Arthur, and then I can come down here and we can work." Oliver glanced over at the door leading into the kitchen. "That is, if it is all acceptable with your Miss Barnsley. As well as everyone else. I know that this in your space not mine, and I don't want to intrude in any way."

Miss Barnsley appeared at the doorway almost instantly. "I'm sure we can work something out, Mr Guildman. As long as you have Mr Pennington's approval."

Oliver nodded. "Of course. I'll ask him first thing tomorrow. It should have no effect on Arthur's education or Isabella's work, so I cannot see a reason he should refuse."

"I can see about setting up another small table?" Miss Barnsley asked "Would you need privacy?"

It was Oliver's turn to blush, which Isabella found undeniably charming. "No no, Miss Barnsley. I'm sure we can work around everyone else. I wouldn't want them to feel outed in any way."

"Looks like you're going to need to work out some new endings to your stories, mate." James voice came from out of the kitchen again. "Sounds like our resident storyteller has been whisked away."

Oliver looked to Isabella in panic and guilt. She quickly comforted him. "He's joking, Oliver. Don't worry." Isabella raised her voice and sent it in the direction of the kitchen. "And I'm sure I'll find some time for a story or two. And Carlos's endings are nice, I personally like them!"

"So shall we start tomorrow?" Oliver asked. "Is that enough time Miss Barnsley? It can be later if need be."

"Tomorrow works just fine, Mr Guildman." Miss Barnsley nodded. "We'll have a station set up for you and Isabella."

"Thank you very much." Oliver turned to Isabella. "And thank you, Isabella. I am greatly looking forward to working with you."

"And I with you, Oliver." She smiled.

Oliver extended his hand out for a handshake, and Isabella took it lightly. The two shook hands in agreement, and Oliver took his leave.

Dawn, James, and Carlos made their way back into the common room to finish their dinners, as Isabella sat down to start on hers.

Dawn was looking at Isabella with an amused smirk she had never seen before. "He's got very nice eyes, doesn't he?"

Isabella wasn't quite sure how to respond. Dawn was right, but she knew admitting that would give James far too much material to tease her with.

"I for one am happy for you, Izzy." James said. "Your stories are the best I've heard, and you deserve to excel." Isabella was touched by James surprisingly heartfelt comment. "And also it doesn't hurt that he just so happens to be—"

"All right all right!" Miss Barnsley interrupted, saving Isabella. "It's all quite unconventional, but let's all do our best to accommodate Mr Guildman and Isabella in their academic endeavours." Even Miss Barnsley couldn't help but tinge her final words with a slight subtext. "But this can only happen if you ensure you aren't distracted from any of your responsibilities, Isabella."

"I promise I won't be, Miss Barnsley. I'll make sure I get everything I need to get done before any lessons. I promise."

Miss Barnsley chuckled. "Good luck to you, girl."

CHAPTER 15

Oliver had been correct in his assumption that Mr Pennington would agree to him working with Isabella after hours. Miss Barnsley had found a small table that they were able to set up in the corner of the room, and Oliver and Isabella started the very next evening.

At first Oliver simply spent time finding out what Isabella was already aware of. In many cases, it turned out she had instinctually picked up on many of the conventions of storytelling and grammar, without being conscious of it. How he was able to help was in pointing them out to her. "Good writers always break rules." Oliver had commented one evening. "But to be able to properly break rules, you must properly know them first." He never spoke down to or infantilised Isabella, and was always just as interested in her views and ideas on things alongside any literary criticisms they would discuss.

One thing they shared was a love for Bentley Miscellany, and whenever a new issue came out, they would spend that evening's session reviewing all of the various stories included in that volume.

Soon, the two of them started to work on pieces of their

own, as opposed to simply discussing others. Oliver was of the belief that the best way to learn was to apply what has been taught, and he thought Isabella was a perfect example of this. At first she felt quite embarrassed by how messy and juvenile her handwriting was compared with his honed calligraphy, but Oliver quickly dissuaded her trepidation, saying one's handwriting was only ever as good as the words they were writing, and in Isabella's case, the words were very very good.

Oliver also extended the same amount of respect and care when it came to all of the other staff members. He learnt all their names, and would partake in small talk before and after sessions. All of them came to respect and like him too. Carlos even started to prepare an extra plate of dinner so that he could share with them. In fact, for some of their sessions, Isabella and Oliver decided to forgo the separate table for discussion, and would include anyone else who was eating at that time — these would usually evolve into Isabella telling a story, with some aid and support from Oliver.

He also always made sure to help in tidying up after the meals as well, a quality that Miss Barnsley took an instant shining towards him for. "A man with a good mind, is only worthy of one if he also has a good heart. And a man who cleans up after himself, well, that's as good a heart as one can ask for, isn't it?" Isabella couldn't agree more with Miss Barnsley. Not only was Oliver teaching her so much about writing and storytelling, but he also was one of the kindest and most respectful people she had ever met.

"He sounds like a very charming and respectful young man." Aunt Maggie commented during dinner. Isabella was staying over for the night, as it was a day off for her, and she had been updating her Aunt on all the happenings within the house and especially her work with Oliver. "I'm very glad you've found someone else who you can work and grow with."

"Someone else?" Isabella hadn't even realised how everything must have sounded to Aunt Maggie. "I didn't mean it to come across like that at all, Aunt! No one could ever replace you."

Aunt Maggie smiled. "No I know you don't, Izzy. It's just surreal for me to see you growing up. You are so much like your mother..." Isabella wasn't sure how to respond. It had been so long now — almost ten years — since her mother had passed away: Aunt Maggie felt more like her mother. "She would have been so proud of you."

"And I'm sure she would have been so thankful to you, coming in and raising me." Isabella said.

"Perhaps..." Aunt Maggie looked off into a distance in her mind. "Some things we will never get a chance to settle until we reach Heaven I suppose." She let out a sigh, and then changed her tone to become more upbeat again. "Anyways, other than the intelligent handsome young man who is giving you a lot of attention, what else is going on in the household? How is Miss Vanessa and her children? Are they all settled in?"

"Miss Vanessa brings Mr Pennington so much joy." Isabella begun. "She's a really lovely woman from the short time that I've known her. Her daughter Lola keeps to herself a lot, I barely even see her, but I think she's comfortable enough. Mr Pennington adores her too." Isabella couldn't help but laugh as she talked about the twins next. "The twins are... the twins. They supersede any description I can give them. But they are lovely. A bit hectic at times, but such kind souls. Always having such fun, they still see the world as so bright." Isabella pondered on the difference between siblings for a moment. "I think Lola was old enough to really know her father before he died, the twins didn't as they were so young, so their sense of loss is a lot less overbearing, I guess. I'm not sure." It struck Isabella how close to home Lola's own experience must be to hers in many ways.

"And how is that Arthur boy taking it?" Aunt Maggie gently

interrupted Isabella's train of thought. "A new mother and siblings is a lot for a fourteen year old only child."

"He's fifteen now, I believe." Isabella said. "And…" Isabella was about to simply say he was doing fine too, but she realised that wasn't entirely the case. "I don't know for sure, but I think he might be finding it quite difficult, even still."

Isabella recalled a time only in the past week where she had overhead Mr Pennington and his son arguing in the study room. She was out in the hallway, so couldn't always pick out the words, but it sounded very heated, with Arthur raising his voice on multiple occasions. One phrase that rang out clearly was "That was mother's! And Vanessa isn't mother so she shouldn't have it!" Isabella wasn't sure what he was referring to, but the sentiment was clear. Arthur clearly saw Vanessa as a replacement for his mother, and he was rejecting her. As Isabella continued to dust, she froze as the door to the study room opened. Arthur stormed through, tears of anger streaming down his cheeks. The next person to emerge out of the doorway surprised Isabella: it was Miss Vanessa herself. She had streaks down her cheeks that was evidence she had been crying as well. Isabella did her best not to stare and become conspicuous. Mr Pennington embraced his wife in an attempt to comfort her.

"He'll come around, I'm sure of it." He said quietly.

"I don't know, Robert. I hope he does. I'm trying, I really am."

"I know, my darling. I know."

Isabella shook the memory from the front of her mind, it wasn't a pleasant one. "Things will all be well in the end I'm sure."

"Mhmm." Aunt Maggie hummed in agreement.

"I'm also starting to write a book." Isabella said, changing the subject.

Aunt Maggie's eyebrows raised in surprise. "A book?"

"Yes." Isabella nodded. "A full one. A novel I mean. Or at

least, something longer than anything I've written before. I just feel like it's the next natural step for me and my craft." Isabella felt silly for calling what she did a craft, but Oliver had encouraged her to view her skill in a more favourable light: "You're more talented than a lot of people who get published, Isabella. I say you own your talent, be proud of it."

"That is an exciting venture." Aunt Maggie said. "A big but exciting one."

"I know! But I'm sure with all that you have taught me over so many years of incredible stories now, and the guidance and teachings that Oliver has given me, I'm more than ready to at least make a first attempt."

"Does Mr Guildman know about your decision to write a novel?"

Isabella shook her head. "Not yet. I wanted to tell you first." This elicited a smile from her Aunt. "See? Haven't replaced you at all."

"I am always here for you, my Amazing Izzy." Aunt Maggie raised her cup in toast to Isabella, and the two finished off their dinner contently.

CHAPTER 16

"*A* novel?" Oliver's eyebrows raised in much the same way Aunt Maggie's had. "That's... An incredible idea!" He let out a laugh of joy. "I am always here to help in any way you'd like."

"I was thinking I might just work on it as a personal thing at first." Isabella admitted. "Just in case it does horrible crash and burn."

"Of course, it's your own personal thing." Oliver said. "Though I'm sure it won't crash and burn. I look forward to reading it some day."

"I don't know what I'll do with it when it's done." Isabella said sheepishly. "I think I'm doing it more for myself than anyone else. Just so I know that I've done it. I've written a novel."

"At the end of the day, the only person we can ever truly write for is ourselves." Oliver quipped.

And that's exactly what Isabella did. Over the next couple months, Isabella started to scrawl down and brainstorm ideas for a long overarching story — like Oliver Twist that had gotten her in Bentley's Miscellany. She sometime daydreamed about sending it off to Richard Bentley once it was complete and getting it published, but she quickly dismissed those ideas. The story pulled elements from her own experience, but also from the experiences of all the people around her. She didn't want to simply write something purely autobiographical — and to create something truly worthy of feeling like a saga, she would need to pull from more than simply her own life anyway. She had some of the most fun when being able to embellish moments with pure fiction. The catharsis and structure that writing afforded her was endlessly fascinating.

For the most part she worked on it by herself. She did pitch some of the new story moments to her Aunt, and Oliver was always happy to help with sentence structure and any grammatical questions she may have, but both of them understood that this was something Isabella wanted — and perhaps had to — do for herself.

Isabella's favourite character to write for and about quickly became a young woman named Nora. It took her quite awhile to realise, but it came as a revelation to Isabella: Nora was Isabella's stand in for Nancy, her old friend from the orphanage. She finally was telling their story, though perhaps not in the way either of the two girls had expected when they had made that pact.

CHAPTER 17

"You're going where?" Isabella asked in confusion.

Oliver had come down into the servant common room to find her, this time in the morning hours as opposed to around dinner time.

"Well, I told Mr Pennington I could take Arthur out for a field trip of sorts." Oliver began to explain. "To a place called 'The Temple of Muses'. In the centre, and it's the largest bookstore that I've ever been to. It's truly incredible."

"That sounds wonderful." Isabella said. "I hope it cheers him up at least a little."

"Mr Pennington requested I take Lola along too. I think just to give her a chance for some fresh air and a change in scenery." Oliver continued. "And I asked Mr Pennington if I could quote 'bring another adult with me to make sure they're both safe' unquote." Oliver grinned.

It took a second for everything to line up for Isabella, but when it finally did, excitement flooded her. "And you asked if I could come along too?"

"I did indeed. And he, of course, said yes." Oliver smile had already told of Mr Pennington's agreement, but it only heightened the excitement to hear Oliver say it out loud. "So, if Miss Barnsley can spare you for the day, I would love for you to come along with us to The Temple of Muses. Strictly for babysitting purposes, of course." His last comment was purely satirical.

"Yes, that's fine, Mr Guildman!" Miss Barnsley called from somewhere. Isabella wasn't sure where Miss Barnsley was, let alone how she had overhead the conversation. I guess when you're in charge of keeping a house in check, you learn to keep an eye on it.

Isabella leapt forward and hugged Oliver in gratitude. "Thank you so much! I don't know how I can ever repay you." Oliver froze up, his hands staying at his side in surprise. As quickly as she had pulled in, Isabella pushed out. Her face went crimson in embarrassment. "Sorry... I..."

"No no, it's absolutely fine." Oliver said, his face also reddening to a light shade of pink. "I am very glad that you're excited. I can't wait for you to see it. It'll take your breath away I'm sure."

∽

THE JOURNEY into the centre of London had gone smoothly enough. Arthur hadn't been very forthcoming in speaking to anyone about anything. Lola was quite quiet around Mr Guildman and Arthur, but when Isabella had started talking to her alone, the two had gotten on quite well.

It turned out that Lola spent a lot of her time reading herself. It was one of the ways to pass the time in an enjoyable way that could be done at one's own pace. Isabella was overjoyed to hear of another bookworm, and found herself suggesting quite a few different literary magazines to Lola.

"You're the maid that Mr Guildman writes with, aren't you?" Lola asked.

Isabella stammered. She wasn't sure how many people knew

about her and Oliver's arrangement, and she also wasn't sure how much the arrangement relied on staying unknown. If too many people, or the wrong person, found out, Oliver might want to cease their meetings. "I, well. Mr Guildman is very good at what he teaches, and I have a passing interest in it all, but I wouldn't say that—"

Lola smiled and cut Isabella's rambling off. "You don't need to worry about me Miss Farmerson. I'm not going to run and tell, if that's what you're worried about. My step-father already knows anyways."

Isabella took a breath of relief. "Feel free to call me Isabella, Miss..." Isabella wasn't sure which family name to use.

"Lola." Lola said. "You can just call me Lola. It's simpler for everyone... Easier too."

"I know what it's like, Lola. Losing a parent." Isabella said tenderly. "I understand how hard it is. You're doing such a great job at staying strong."

Lola's eyes widened in surprise, but before anything more could be said, the two were interrupted by Oliver announcing: "We're here!"

Oliver had been right. The Temple of Muses did take Isabella's breath away. As soon as they entered the building, Isabella was overcome with just how big the place was — and how many books it held. There was a large circular counter in the middle of the main area, which several clerks were working behind, packaging up various books for customers.

"Some say this area is so large, a mail-coach drawn by four horses could fit and drive around in here." Oliver stated. "Though whether that's actually true, I couldn't say. I haven't got a coach to spare at the moment." Lola and Isabella smiled at his joke. Arthur was barely paying attention.

Isabella let her eyes wandered over what seemed like never ending shelves. Each shelf containing more books than Isabella had ever seen in one place ever. Mr Pennington's shelves had impressed her; these shelves left her in awe.

"Feel free to look around." Oliver said to them all. Arthur started to aimlessly wander, dragging his finger absentmindedly along the spines of the books. Lola cautiously went searching on her own, though she always stayed within view of Oliver and Isabella.

"It's incredible." Isabella said to Oliver. He smiled.

"It's one of the most wonderful places in the world." He said. "So many stories, birthed from so many minds. So many different walks of life, so many different points of view. They're all here. All just at our fingertips." He looked up at one of the tallest shelves. "Well, some perhaps require a ladder to get too." He and Isabella chuckled.

"Thank you for bringing me along." Isabella said.

"Of course." Oliver glanced over at Arthur. "I feel like you'll get more out of this than my student. Not quite sure how to reach him..." Oliver sighed. "But anyways. I wanted you to see this place. Who knows, maybe one of your stories will end up here one day!"

Isabella laughed at Oliver's comment, dismissing it as mere fantasy, but she could feel the dream alight in her heart. *Maybe one day.*

"Why do you teach, Oliver?" Isabella found herself asking. Perhaps to pull the spotlight away from herself.

"Oh wow..." Oliver considered how he should answer for a moment. "I think I teach because... Seeing someone excel at something they've been created for, is far more exciting to me than any achievement I could make on my own. I would rather be helping someone else scale their mountain, than just be standing at the top of the peak by myself." Oliver turned to look at Isabella. "I do have to say, your mountain has been a particularly fascinating one to climb with you. Though I'm not sure how much help I've really been."

"You have helped and taught me so much." Isabella realised she was now staring deep into Oliver's hazel eyes, and he was staring back. They stood there for a moment, surrounded by the endless sea of stories, taking in each other. Isabella noticed Oliver's mouth open slightly, as if he was about to say something, but he didn't.

"Can I get this?" The moment was broken and passed. Oliver and Isabella turned to see Lola holding a small book in her hand. "Father gave me some spending money, I can use that."

"A wonderful choice, Miss Pennington." Oliver said, clearing his throat and taking a small step away from Isabella.

He went over to the counter with Lola to aid in purchasing the book, leaving Isabella to stew in what had just occurred.

She had always known that Oliver was a handsome man, it was clear to anyone, but that had never been a prevailing thought in her mind — until today. Not only was he handsome, but he was so kind and selfless and intelligent. The thought of the two of them forging a life together, telling each other stories, telling their children—

Isabella cut herself off. Oliver was a tutor, a well-respected young man, and she was a maid. It could never be. Isabella had learnt from her gruelling year at the orphanage that yearning for something unattainable does no one any good. Be grateful in the good already in your life, and don't covet what is not yours. Oh but how she wished...

"Arthur!" Oliver's stern cry broke Isabella how of her short trance. She turned to see that Arthur had exited the store. He was framed by one of grand windows, and was kicking at the pigeons that were gathering on the street outside. Isabella went over to Oliver at the counter, who was lightly frowning at the boy who apparently couldn't — or perhaps was deciding not to — hear him.

"I'll finish up here with Lola." Isabella said. "You can go outside and look after Arthur."

Oliver flashed her a thankful smile, and strode out of the store. Embarrassingly nodding at the doorman.

"I sometimes understand Arthur…" Lola said quietly. "He's lost his mother. I know if I ever lost my mother I would be… But I lost my father, but I don't try and terrorise the world like he does. Is it different, losing a mother rather than a father do you think?"

"I lost both my parents." Isabella was surprised she had admitted that so freely. "Losing either hurts incredibly. I think it may be less about who we lose, and more about how we decide to react and use the feelings that come with that loss."

Lola's eyes widened in surprise. "I had no idea! I'm so sorry. I would never have asked you if I knew."

"It's okay." Isabella found herself smiling at the girl's gentleness. "When I lost my parents, I had a very good friend that I could always talk to. She helped me through so much of my pain. And then my Aunt took me in and helped me too." She lightly took Lola's hand. "I am always here to talk to Lola, about anything. If I can help in any way, please just let me know."

Lola smiled. "Now I see why Mr Guildman made sure to bring you along."

"Why's that?"

"Because you're not just beautiful on the outside, but on the inside as well."

CHAPTER 18

The brief moment she had shared with Oliver, as well as Lola's incredibly kind words, stuck with Isabella for many days after their trip to the Temple of Muses. She replayed the moments in her head over and over — as she was dusting the living room's mantlepiece, as she was mopping the front hallway, even as she sat and wrote her book: *beautiful, both inside and out*.

Isabella had given up trying to scold herself for girlish daydreams. She was a storyteller after all, why couldn't she spend a few days in a fantasy of her own? She knew she would get through it, the poignancy of the moment would pass, and she would be fine. At least, she hoped it would pass. At the moment, the feeling of electricity she felt when she and Oliver locked eyes could be recalled and felt again with the same intensity just from the mere thought of it.

"The memories that always feel like yesterday," Aunt Maggie had said once, "are always my favourite. Whether they be good or bad, happy or sad, the fact that you can just reach out and touch them, they're that real still, means those are the moments that define who we are." Isabella wasn't sure what it said about her, that this was a supposedly defining moment for her.

She didn't let any of her musings distract her from both her work for the household, or her work on her book. The novel was coming along nicely. She had filled pages and pages brainstorming ideas for the story and characters, and had moved onto writing the actual prose. The adventures of Nora as she grew up and travelled all over the country — the travelling was an embellishment Isabella had made mixed in with the more autobiographical elements — was taking real shape. She had imagined the story as five parts, and had already written out the first three. The fourth part was the darkest in her plan, and perhaps she was struggling a little to get into that mindset when her thoughts were filled with such joyful memories at the moment.

It was in one of these moments of juxtaposition between uplifting thoughts and dower prose, that Isabella was ambushed by Arthur. She was sitting in the servant's common room, scrawling away with a pencil, when Arthur's shrill voice broke the comfortable silence.

"What are you doing?" He asked, as he entered the room from the upstairs door.

Isabella jumped, instinctually covering the paper with her forearm. "Sorry, Arthur, I didn't see you there. What was that?"

"It's Master Pennington to you, maid." Arthur said, taking a step into the room. "And I said, what are you doing?"

"My apologies, Master Pennington." Isabella stood up in attempt to seem more respectful. There was a strange spite in Arthur's tone that she hadn't heard before, and it sounded dangerous. "I have finished my work for the day, and was just spending some time relaxing before supper."

"Relaxing? Looks like you were writing." Arthur said. "Never really found writing to be very relaxing."

"Yes, well... Sometimes I do. It takes my mind off of things." Isabella felt like she was walking on eggshells already.

"Many maids write, from your experience?" Arthur asked patronisingly. "Do many even read for that matter?"

"I..." Isabella wasn't sure how she should respond, or whether Arthur even wanted her to.

"I can't think it can be many." Arthur continued. "Which would make you what? Better than most of them. In your own eyes at least."

"I don't think that at all." Isabella said. "I've been lucky enough to receive an education, that's all. It doesn't make me any better or worse than anyone else."

"Hmmm." Arthur stroked his chin in mock thought. "I'm not quite sure if I believe you there."

"Well it's the truth." Isabella felt annoyance rising in her. She respected Arthur as the master's son, but she wouldn't be played around with like a cat would play with a mouse.

"Is that why you insist on fraternising with my tutor, maid?" The spite in Arthur's voice raised. "Because you think you're better than everyone else?"

Isabella was dumbfounded.

"Because don't think I haven't noticed." Arthur said. "I knew from that first moment you interrupted my lesson, which should have gotten you kicked out of here in the first place, that you were a wanton woman. Is that why you decided to sink your claws into Mr Guildman? To prove that you could. To prove that you're better than me? That you're smarter than me? Because you're not!"

"What?" Isabella wouldn't be insulted, but she also knew that if she raised her voice, or tried to throw anything back at Arthur, that she wouldn't have a leg to stand on. She tried to keep her breathing steady and her mind calm. "Master Pennington, nothing I have ever done has been to try and spite you or prove that I'm smarter. And I don't know what you've seen or heard to make you believe that I have been fraternising with Oli- With Mr Guildman, but you have wildly misunderstood our arrangement."

"Ah!" Arthur clicked his finger and pointed at Isabella accusatorially. "But there is an arrangement. An arrangement between a tutor and a maid. *My* tutor, and *my* maid."

"I am Mr Pennington's maid, *Master* Pennington." Isabella let her anger take control for just a moment with that jab, but quickly tried to reel herself back in. "Mr Guildman assured me that any work we did was outside of your lesson times, and wouldn't detract from any of your learning. If we could discuss it with him, I'm sure we—"

"What? You want him here so you can flutter your eyelashes at him again, and he'll take you to some magical book store, and drag me along to suffer?" Arthur scoffed. "No no. I think you've seen quite enough of Mr Oliver Guildman. Quite enough indeed."

"Master Pennington." Isabella kept her voice level. "I am sorry for any offence you might have taken from me, and I do admit I was uncouth to interrupt your lesson those many months ago, but I don't believe what Mr Guildman does in his free time should be a concern to you. And if your worry is that I am being improper with him, I can dissuade those fears. Everything between us is strictly professional. Any of the other staff here will stand by that too."

Arthur seemed stumped for a moment. Perhaps he had been expecting Isabella to launch into an aggressive defence of some kind, which he could pin as guilt, but he hadn't prepared for a logical, calm, and tactful reply.

"If you would like for us to talk with your father about this—"

"No no." Arthur interrupted her. "No need to bring my father into this. He's already been distracted himself by some doxy, who's only gone and brought their whole troupe of waifs into my house. Did you know it was the twin's birthdays last week? Got the whole house draped in garish decorations. My mother would have had a fit!"

So that's what's trigged this. Isabella thought to herself, though she didn't voice her realisation. The teenage boy's emotions were running high, and in desperation to expel his own feelings of hurt and loss, he was taking it out on her.

It took every part of Isabella's self-control, but she decided to feel pity and empathy for the boy, and to try and reach out to him; to give him aid in some way. "I lost my mother too, Arthur. I know how hard it is. How unfair life can seem because of it. We have people ripped out of our lives, before we can even truly appreciate how important they are to us."

For a moment, Isabella thought she had got through to Arthur. His eyes had become moist as tears started to form, and he didn't speak. She took a step towards him, but he backed away, wiping his eyes with the back of his forearm.

"I couldn't care less about what you've been through, maid. That is of no concern to me. I am here because you are blatantly abusing the privileged position you are in. If you want to talk about unfairness and injustice, that's what we should be talking about! It's no wonder you didn't have a mother though. With the way you act, it's no surprise."

Isabella wanted to slap the boy. How dare he talk to her like that! She had done her best to understand him, and had even opened herself up and been vulnerable to try and reach him, but he had practically spat in her face!

Her fury was interrupted by a call from the kitchen. "You all right in there, Isabella!" Miss Barnsley called. "Is that you and Mr Oliver working on your book again?"

Arthur's eyes flicked from the source of Miss Barnsley's voice, the papers on the table, and Isabella. "What book is she talking about?"

"Nothing." Isabella said quickly.

"Is that what that is?" Arthur took a step towards the papers on the table, but Isabella scooped them up. He couldn't touch them. He had no right getting into Isabella's personal things.

"It is of no concern to you." Isabella said coldly.

Arthur seemed to take this as a challenge. "Is that so? Because it sounds like that is something which could be pulling my tutor's attention away from me and my very integral education. A promiscuous young maid, distracting a tutor with fantastical little children stories she's writing, making sure she get's back at those who just so happen to be above her in any way."

"Like I said, I don't mean to—"

"Show it to me." Arthur demanded.

"No."

"You're saying no? To me?"

"It isn't for you to see."

"I think I can decide what is and isn't for me, thank you very much. And I certainly can't be told that by the likes of you."

Arthur took a lunge towards Isabella. She dodged to the left, and he went sprawling into the table. He grunted in surprise and pain, before collecting himself.

"How dare you!" He cried out. "Why for that, I ought to—"

"Ought to what?" A voice cut Arthur off. Both he and Isabella turned to see who had spoken.

It was Lola, standing in the doorway. There was a look of determination locked on her face, and her voice held an authority Isabella had never heard from her before.

"Lola, what are you doing here?"

"Father needs you. So I came looking." Lola's voice was level and strong.

"So you came looking where the servants are?" Arthur scoffed again.

"I could hear you." Lola said. "Your voice was raised. I hope you weren't giving Isabella any trouble."

"Isabella?" Arthur turned to Isabella. "You got your hooks in her too already? Fast work."

"She not's got her hooks in anyone, Arthur." Lola took the power again, talking to Arthur with a tone you would use telling off a small child. "She's just personable. You should try it some time, though I'm not sure how well you'd take to it."

Arthur's mouth opened and closed in surprise. He wasn't used to being insulted to his face, and especially not by someone as meek as Lola.

"You don't want to keep father waiting." Lola said flatly.

"I won't keep *my* father waiting." Arthur finally said. He gave Isabella one final scowl, and then started to stalk out. He paused when he passed Lola to say: "He will hear about this!"

Lola didn't dignify his threat with a response, and simply waited until he had gone, slamming the door behind him.

"I hope he wasn't giving you any trouble." Lola said to Isabella.

"He's just a hurting young man." Isabella said, suppressing any spiteful comments she could make. "He seems to think I've been fraudulent with my position, and fraternising with Mr Guildman."

"He can't possibly actually believe that!" Lola said. "No one could think that of you!"

"It seems he does." Isabella sat, and started flatten out the papers that had crumpled in her grasp. "I'll speak to Oliver about it. Hopefully it's just a passing phase, that will be resolved in no time." Isabella looked up at Lola. "Thank you for stepping in. I don't know what would have happened if you hadn't."

"Oh it was nothing." Lola suddenly became the meek shy girl she normally was again. "I just... You're so kind and caring, you don't deserve to be bullied or pushed around at all by anyone." She looked down at the papers Isabella had finished smoothing out. "Is that your book?"

"You know about my book?"

"Oh, well." Lola's face reddened. "I just overheard you and Mr Guildman speaking together at the bookshop, about him saying you could have a story there one day. So I assumed you must have a book, or be working on one."

Isabella paused for a moment, considering whether to let Lola in. "Yes. It's my book."

"I would love to read it when it's finished." Lola said.

"If I'm happy with it, of course you can read it when it's done."

"Why wouldn't you be happy with it? If Mr Guildman is taking time out his evenings to help you pursue your craft, you must be very good at it."

It was Isabella's turn to blush. "I don't know. I wouldn't be able to say really. It is incredibly hard to be your own critic."

"Too easy on yourself?"

Isabella shook her head. "Most of the time, you're too harsh. It's why having likeminded and intelligent people to help you is always important." She smiled up at Lola. "So that is why I'm very grateful I have Oliver and you."

Lola beamed. "Well I can't wait for you to finish it!"

Isabella suddenly had a sinking feeling. What if Arthur's mood didn't pass? What if his threats weren't empty? She would have to talk to Oliver about it. Her world, which had become so comfortable, was now perhaps balancing on a tightrope and a strong gust of wind was coming.

CHAPTER 19

The next day, Isabella told Oliver what happened with Arthur: The ambush and the stand-off. Oliver listened quietly and seriously.

When she was finished recounting the scenario he spoke. "I'm sorry that he was like that with you Isabella. Arthur is…" It took him a moment to find the right words. "He's a very scared boy. He feels lost without his mother in many ways, in the shadow of his father. I'm not saying that gives him the right to mistreat you, but it might explain some of his attitude."

Isabella nodded. "I had thought as much. That's why I tried reaching out to him, showing I understand."

"Sometimes, the only person that can start them on the path of healing is themselves." Oliver mused. "I've also tried reaching out to him, but other than as a tutor, he doesn't want my aid or ear."

"Do you think he'll do anything?" Isabella asked. "About me and what he thinks I've been doing? Do you think he'll tell Mr Pennington."

"Tell him a lie? I don't think so. Arthur is emotional, but he isn't vindictive. I'm sure it's all smoke. He's just puffing out his chest to try and seem big because he feels so small."

Isabella wasn't so sure, but she decided to trust Oliver. After all, he had known the boy longer. On top of that, she simply hoped he was right. Isabella loved her place here at the house, the working conditions were exemplar, all the staff were friendly, she was able to see her Aunt very often and she even earned enough to be able to send some of her wages back to Aunt Maggie, and it gave her access to Oliver and the writing techniques he had been and continued to teach her. She didn't want her life to be upended yet again, not when she was finally comfortable.

Isabella prayed that Oliver was right, and Arthur wouldn't do anything more. Unfortunately, Oliver was wrong.

CHAPTER 20

A tense two weeks passed, and nothing happened. Arthur hadn't seem to report any misdemeanour, and he even seemed to be more friendly to both Oliver and even Isabella.

She did her best to stay out of his way the best she could, and to make sure that she was extremely proper with Oliver when outside of the servant common room. She felt frustrated that she had to overcorrect herself because of the emotional whims of a child, but she didn't want to jeopardise her place, and if this is what it took to keep the boy's temper at ease, then this is what she would do.

Oliver also had lightly probed Arthur about Isabella, but Arthur hadn't revealed anything. On the surface, it looked like the storm had passed, and the boy had moved on.

Even still, Isabella couldn't shake the feeling that something was going to shift in her life again. She prayed about it, asking for the anxiety to be taken from her, or if it was there for a reason, for that reason to be shown to her.

The reason came on a cool Tuesday afternoon, when Isabella was called once again into Mr Pennington's study, just as she had over a year ago now. That time, he had invited her in to offer her a job, this time however...

"Now, Miss Farmerson." Isabella had never heard Mr Pennington so grave and serious. "Some things have been brought to my attention, some very worrying things. You see my son Arthur's education is one of the most important things to me. Making sure that he has the skills needed to make it in this world, maybe even take over from me one day, is of upmost importance." Isabella felt like her chest was filled with rocks, as she sunk into the chair she was sitting in. Mr Pennington had her sit across from him at his desk this time, not on the more comfortable lounge chairs by the fireplace. "And I'm hearing from him, that some of your actions are causing his education to wane. Your actions concerning Mr Guildman."

Isabella wasn't sure if Mr Pennington was waiting for a reply. She opened her mouth to defend herself, but Mr Pennington continued before she could even muster a single word.

"I can appreciate that Mr Guildman is a very attractive and charming young gentleman." Mr Pennington adjusted his tie. "But that is no excuse for any sort of fraternisation. Of any kind."

Isabella still waited, not wanting to interrupt. This time though, Mr Pennington raised his eyebrows, and she felt the invite – or perhaps order – to speak. "Mr Pennington, firstly I want to begin with how grateful I am for the position you have given me, and how well I have been treated."

Mr Pennington brow furrowed. "It sounds like you have been perhaps a little too grateful."

"I can assure you, whatever your son has said, Mr Guildman and I have not done anything improper or untoward, and on top of that, there has been no instance where either of us felt that any of the work that we have been doing together has inhibited Arthur's education in any way. His education has always and will always be Mr Guildman's first priority."

Mr Pennington lifted up some sheets of paper, and turned them round so that Isabella could see them. "This would suggest otherwise, Miss Farmerson."

She leant forward to inspect them closer. She quickly recognised Oliver's hand writing: this was some of Arthur's work that had been marked and corrected. Even from just a quick glance it was evident that the marks were low and the quality of the work was all over the place. Isabella was shocked. Arthur had never been a complete natural when it came to academic work, but he had never been this rough.

Arthur must have purposefully started to sabotage some of his own work. Isabella thought to herself as she looked over the different worksheets. *That's why he hasn't said anything for two weeks. He was building up a dossier of evidence to condemn me with!* It was a plan almost dastardly enough for a villain in one of Isabella's stories.

"Mr Pennington..." Isabella started cautiously. "I think what may have happened here is—"

"No no! Miss Farmerson." Mr Pennington raised a hand to stop her talking. She was so surprised her mouth hung open for a couple seconds longer than she would like before she could remember to shut it. "Arthur has warned me of how you can use your words to twist any situation into your favour. I've heard enough from him to understand. I've not brought you in to have you attempt to vindicate yourself, Miss Farmerson. I've brought you in as a courtesy, to let you know that you must leave us privately. I could make a big show and example of you, but you have always been a very dedicated maid, up until recently it seems."

Isabella's blood ran cold. She hadn't expected to be thrown to the street.

"No!" A voice cried out from behind the door. It suddenly

burst open, and Lola came rushing in. She must have been pressed up against it, listening in. "Father! You mustn't send Isabella away! She hasn't done what Arthur accuses her of! It isn't true."

Isabella rose to try and calm the hysterical girl. Lola ran into her arms, tears streaming down her face. Isabella didn't worry about her position in the house for a moment, and just focused on holding the girl.

"Please..." Lola said. Isabella wasn't sure if it was to her or to Mr Pennington. Perhaps it was to both of them. "I can't have her go away too."

Mr Pennington stood up, and leant on his desk. His expression was dark, and Isabella turned her body so that Lola wasn't able to see it. "I see you've already turned my daughter against me... Perhaps in preparation for when you were caught out?"

"Mr Pennington, I have done no such thing. Lola loves you, and—"

"Isabella is the only one here who understands me!" Lola pulled out from the embrace and faced her step-father. She wiped the tears from her cheeks with the backs of her sleeves. "She is the kindest and most patient person I have ever met, and if you send her away, it'll be the biggest mistake you ever make!"

Mr Pennington was taken aback by Lola's bold statements. Isabella had learnt two weeks ago that Lola had a real fire in her, but this was the first time Mr Pennington had witnessed it.

For a moment, it seemed like Mr Pennington was considering Lola's words, but a glance down at the papers — the apparent evidence that his son was falling behind, supposedly because of Isabella — reinforced his resolve. His voice went cold, almost disconnected from his conscious or humanity. "I'm sorry Lola, but I just cannot risk Arthur's future. For any reason. For anyone." He locked eyes with Isabella, his expression steel. "Miss Farmerson, I would like you to go downstairs, and pack your bag. My decision has been made and is final. I know you have your Aunt, so you won't be slumming on the streets tonight." He took a pause. "I do want you to know, this doesn't please me in any way. I am just as hurt and disappointed as you are. I truly am. But you must understand, I cannot risk my son's future."

Isabella wanted to say more. There must be something she can do, something to prove her innocence. But the more she tried to find an avenue to go down, the more she realised: there was nothing she could do. She would just have to do what she was told; she would have to pack her bags, and leave.

A small shred of hope still glistened in the darkness of despair though. *If Oliver can plead my case...* Isabella couldn't count on it though. Arthur would probably find some way to discredit Oliver's word as he had with hers.

Isabella nodded, held back the tears, and went to leave the room without another word. Lola grasped at her hand and wouldn't let go though. She turned to Lola, and did her best to smile.

"Please, don't go." Lola whispered. "I need you. You're the only one who can make the world make sense."

"No." Isabella whispered back, very aware that Mr Pennington was watching them with a severe look. "You could always make sense of it yourself, you just needed me to nudge you in the right direction. You have that direction now, Lola."

"But why can't that be the same direction as you?"

"This isn't a fairytale..." Isabella said sadly, as Lola finally let go of her hand. "Not everything makes sense. I'm sorry." Isabella quickly turned and fled the room. She could feel the tears bombarding against her eyes, and she knew she wouldn't be able to hold them in any longer.

As soon as she was out of the study, she began to weep. She ran quickly downstairs, hoping she wouldn't bump into anyone. Luckily she didn't.

She made her way into her room, and started to pack a small

THE ORPHAN PRODIGY'S STOLEN TALE

bag of belongings. Packing through tears, her blood ran cold for the second time that hour.

Her book was gone.

The packing was put on hold, as Isabella started to furiously search around her room for the notebooks that held the thousands of words she had assembled, but it was no where to be seen.

Arthur's taken it. Isabella scolded herself for jumping to such an accusation without any solid proof, but she couldn't help herself. Her despair gave way into anger. She wanted to scream. She wanted to rail against the world, against Mr Pennington for believing his snivelling liar of a son, and for Arthur for being such an impudent child. Later on, she would regret all the horrible thoughts she had in that moment, but she couldn't help it as her emotions raged.

She probably would have ended up screaming if Miss Barnsley hadn't entered the room at that very moment.

"Isabella." She said. It was clear from the tone of her voice, and the weight of her expression that she had been told.

"You don't believe him, do you?" Isabella pleaded. "You don't think I'm what Arthur says I am?"

"No I don't." Miss Barnsley said. "I know you are one of the most upstanding girls I have ever had the pleasure of working with. And I also voiced my beliefs to Mr Pennington, but..."

"But it wasn't enough. Was it?"

Miss Barnsley shook her head. "Mr Pennington is so set on making sure Arthur's future is secure. To the point that he can become blind to everything else. He's seen so many people get betrayed and stabbed in the back in his line of work, that the paranoia of that has bled into his personal life..."

With each word from Miss Barnsley, Isabella's heart sank lower. She tried to lift a shirt into her bag, but her arms couldn't move. She felt so weak, so powerless.

Miss Barnsley walked over, and just put her arms very gently around her. Isabella was surprised, Miss Barnsley had never been the very affection type, but she welcomed the embrace. She just wanted to be held, even if it was just for a moment.

She spent a few of her last fleeting moments, curled into Miss Barnsley, mourning the life that she had settled into slipping through her fingers no matter how hard she tried to grasp onto it. Yet again, she was being buffeted away to something new, and Isabella was sure it wouldn't be as comfortable and exciting as this one had been.

CHAPTER 21

*A*unt Maggie had accepted Isabella back in, instantly. Isabella had turned up on her doorstep in a flood of tears, and a bag over her shoulder.

Without hesitation, Maggie had taken the bag and set it aside for later, sat her niece down at the table, and made her a nice warm cup of tea. Very slowly and carefully, Aunt Maggie had coaxed the sequence of events from Isabella, how it had come to be that she was shunned out of the household all of a sudden.

Isabella struggled to tell her about the final goodbye she had given to Lola, a tight hug, before leaving the house. She hadn't had a chance to say goodbye to most of the staff, and Oliver hadn't been teaching Arthur that day. As she was recounting the story to her Aunt, the thought hit her: she may never see Oliver again. This revelation made her start crying all over again. She only just managed to finish her tale of woe with, "And my book is gone!"

"What?" Aunt Maggie stopped mid-pour in surprise.

"My book." Isabella sniffed. "The one I've spent months writing. When I went to pack my things, it wasn't there."

"And you think Arthur took it do you?" Aunt Maggie asked.

Isabella nodded. It made her feel better that she wasn't the only one to come to that conclusion. "But I didn't have any way to prove it, so there was nothing I could do."

Aunt Maggie finished pouring her third cup of tea, and sat deep in thought and reflection. "I am so so sorry, Izzy."

"Why are you sorry?" Isabella reached out a hand across the table to her Aunt. "You have always been amazing to me. You're the only person who is constant in my life. The only person I have ever been able to rely on."

Aunt Maggie smiled. She got up to get some small biscuits, but as she began to arise, a hacking cough brought her back to sitting.

Isabella jumped across to her. "Are you okay?" She asked in worry.

"I'm fine. I'm fine." Aunt Maggie cleared her throat and patted Isabella's hand in assurance. "It's just—" She was cut off again by another round of coughs. She pulled out a small handkerchief and coughed into it.

"How long has this been going on for?" Isabella rushed to get her Aunt a glass of water.

"I don't know…" Aunt Maggie admitted. "A couple months now."

"A couple months! Why didn't you tell me!"

"I didn't want to worry you." Aunt Maggie said. "Everything was going so well for you, and I didn't want to be a burden."

"Auntie!" Isabella almost cried out. "You could never be a burden!"

"I should be fine… It's just, with all the cleaning work, I don't have time to rest and recoup. I was so grateful for the money you sent me, but I have to keep working for—"

"Well, that'll change now." Isabella interrupted. "I'm back with you now, and I'll work twice as hard for the both of us. I don't want you working until you're better. Okay?"

Aunt Maggie didn't agree to Isabella's terms, but Isabella hoped that she could at least convince her Aunt to take a short break off work. Now that Isabella was home, she could take over the jobs that Maggie was doing, allowing her Aunt to rest and recover. With two mouths to feed, Isabella knew she would probably need to find a couple more customers to cover all their costs, especially if any medicine was required. Isabella had a small amount of savings — her wages at the Pennington's had been more generous than some — but that would quickly dwindle.

"I'm back now, Aunt." Isabella said, almost more for herself. "Everything will be sorted and fine." She tried to bring a hopeful bounce to her voice. "Should be simple enough, right?"

~

UNFORTUNATELY, things were about as far from simple as they could have been. Isabella set out early the next morning to the first of Aunt Maggie's clients, but when she got there, she was turned away. The same thing happened at the next place, and the next place. Every client on the list turned her away, and all for the same reason: they had all been told about the fraternising maid by Mr Pennington. Some were more cordial with their rejections, simply turning her away with a quiet curt word, but others were not so kind. At one house, the butler stepped out into the street and loudly reprimanded Isabella for her supposed sins; it was unclear whether this man actually knew any of the specifics of Isabella's situation, but that didn't matter to him. He shouted at her, and she fled in tears.

That had been the last name on the clientele list. No one would take her.

There was no way Isabella could allow for her Aunt to go to work in her condition. There was only one option left. It wasn't a desirable path in any way, but it was necessary.

Isabella went and signed up to work in the large paper mill. She had spent so many years working hard, but she had never been in a place like that before.

For the sake of her Aunt, Isabella became a workhouse girl.

CHAPTER 22

*H*er first day in the paper mill reminded Isabella strongly of her first day at the orphanage. A sea of indistinct faces glanced at her in curiosity when she first passed, but would quickly turn away again, focussing back on the gruelling work at hand.

The foreman also had the same streak of cruel strictness that Miss Strawson had possessed, though he seemed a lot more prone to lashing out at anyone who was falling behind with his cane. Isabella made sure to steer as clear of him as she possibly could.

Their job was shredding bundles of rags, making sure to cut away anything such as buttons or hooks. Only pure cotton or linen could go into the rag boilers. This boiled cotton was then sent to the beaters to be crushed and soak in water, which resulted in a sodden white porridge everyone simply just called 'stuff'. That stuff was then sent off to moulds, where further steps were taken — Isabella hadn't worked out quite what yet — and this then resulted in paper. As she was only involved in the shredding steps, Isabella had had to ask questions and carefully observe to work out what happened next. Despite how gruelling the work was, and how poor the conditions, she still was amazed at the process. This was way the blank canvases she had done all of her writing on was made. It was a strange feeling, seeing the very start of it all.

She would have tried harder over the first three weeks of working there to try and find out what happened to the 'stuff' in the moulds, if it weren't for the fact that her days were so long, and she was completely exhausted by the end of them. Her hands were red raw from all the tugging and pulling and tearing she was required to do, as well as littered with small cuts that were unavoidable when shredding and cutting so much so quickly.

This exhaustion seemed to be a universal experience, as almost none of the women spoke to each other. Isabella still hadn't learnt the names of any of them, and it seemed the foreman encouraged this anonymity. Friends chatter to each other and get distracted, mindless nameless machines simply do their work.

No one even made eye contact once everyone was sitting down and working. It was a bizarre wasteland of exhausted husks, simply battling to stay awake until the end of the day. Isabella couldn't even fight back sleep for long enough to exchange stories with her Aunt when she arrived home, though Aunt Maggie seemed much the same, exhausted with battling whatever ailment was troubling her. The thought of continuing to write was completely out of the question, at least for now. Isabella didn't have the mental energy or fortitude for anything other than work.

She had been working tirelessly every day for a month, when she finally spotted the person who had been glancing at her. Isabella had felt it a couple times previously, that strange sensation of being watched, but whenever she had glanced around herself to see if anyone was looking over, she saw nothing but the tops of women's heads, as they looked down at their worktables. This time however, she finally looked up quickly enough to just catch a glimpse of one of the women rapidly looking away.

Isabella lightly frowned, and tried to blink through the fuzziness in her exhausted mind. She didn't recognise her watcher, but there was something oddly familiar, almost nostalgic, about her. The lady's hair was cut short, and was a light mousey brown, though Isabella couldn't tell if that colour was due to the dirt and dust in the air clinging to it. Isabella spent as long as she could risk looking at this mystery woman, before turning back to her work; if she had looked and studied any longer, she surely would have gotten reprimanded by the foreman.

At the end of the day, Isabella rushed out to wait by the exit, hoping to catch the woman and at least ask her name. Maybe there was no connection between the two of them, but a new connection was just as pleasant a thought.

She stood shivering in the cold, the sun having started to set hidden by the buildings already. She could see her breath pluming out in a white mist from her mouth, but she waited. Droves of woman came filing out of the paper mill, but Isabella couldn't see the one she was waiting to speak to.

A cutting breeze seemed to snake its way across Isabella, sending a shock down her spine. She shook it off. The breeze had sent a piece of litter flying across the street and into her leg. Bending down to pick it up, Isabella froze in a different kind of shock. She had simply intended to discard the litter, but she pulled it up to read when she had realised what it was: the latest issue of Bentley's Miscellany.

Isabella couldn't help herself, and opened up the magazine to check the inside contents. Even though the evening was cold, she couldn't help but feel a warm buzz of excitement at the opportunity to read something new. An ache for the life she had lost grew in her chest, but she did her best to repress it. She wanted to be grateful for this small blessing, rather than yearn for more.

Isabella quickly glanced around again as the crowd of workers had started to disperse — still no sign of her mystery woman — and then started to read one of the first entries in the magazine. It was the first part of a multi-part story apparently. Even though she might not get the chance to read the other parts, Isabella was overjoyed she could at least read something.

The joy quickly faded into confusion. As she kept reading, she recognised some of the characters. More than that, she recognised the specific passages. She recognised the writing style. She knew this piece perfectly, word for word.

It was the first part of the novel she was writing.

But how could this be? Her novel had been taken by Arthur Pennington in spite when he had framed her and had her cast out. Unless…

Isabella flipped the pages to check the authorship listed at the end of the piece. The words seemed to laugh at her, as they sat there in stark black ink.

'WRITTEN BY ARTHUR PENNINGTON'

She couldn't believe her eyes. Here were her words, the story she had poured her passion into, printed in her favourite magazine. It was the stuff of dreams. Except everything was all wrong, for the words were being credited to someone else. Arthur had stolen her work, he had stolen her dream!

Without thinking, Isabella began marching across the city to Mr Pennington's house. Her exhaustion had seemingly disappeared, numbed over by the adrenaline of anger. She didn't think of what she would say or do when she reached her destination, she simply powered on through the cold. Something had to be done, surely. This was an injustice. This was a crime!

The walk took her the better part of an hour, even at the pace she was storming at, but it allowed her some time to cool off. By the time she had reached the road of the Pennington's establishment, the red had disappeared from her vision, and her thoughts could race more clearly.

So I'm here. Isabella mused to herself. *But what am I to do when I reach the door? Knock, demand admittance and accuse Arthur of plagiarism, of theft. Then what? Mr Pennington has already proven he will side with his son over anyone, even when proof can be presented.* There was no point storming up to the door. *And what about if I took it elsewhere? Told the police or... Who would believe the words of a shamed Millhouse girl against the word of a wealthy man?*

All hope and fight left Isabella's body, and she collapsed down on the street opposite the door to the Pennington's. There was nothing she could do, but clutch the magazine in her hand, and stare at the life she had not only lost, but the dream that had been taken from her.

Maybe Oliver would be leaving soon? Perhaps she could finally see him, see him again after all the chaos that had been this past month, he would have a solution. Oliver would know how to set things right. Even if he didn't, Isabella missed him bitterly. A few moments with Oliver could make her feel so much better, she knew that to be true.

So she waited.

And waited.

But Oliver did not come.

The sun had well and truly set now, and the moon was full in the sky, illuminating Isabella in her despair.

Her eyelids felt like they had great anchors attached to them, and Isabella could feel sleep fighting to take over. She had almost drifted off when she heard the sound of the door opening. She shook herself awake and stood up.

It wasn't Oliver, but Miss Barnsley that was on the doorstep. "Isabella? Is that you?" Miss Barnsley asked.

Isabella pulled herself up to standing. "Yes, Miss Barnsley. It's me."

"I..." Miss Barnsley seemed lost for words. Isabella had never seen her so embarrassed before. "What are you doing here, dearest? Mr Pennington hasn't changed his mind."

"I know." Isabella said cooly. "But he has seemed to change the mind of anyone looking for a cleaner." That comment felt slightly uncalled for, but Isabella was tired and hungry and angry. "But I'm not here for Mr Pennington. I'm looking for Mr Guildman."

"Mr Guildman?" Miss Barnsley shook her head. "He's not been here today, dear. He had some personal business to attend to apparently, couldn't come."

"Has he..." Isabella couldn't finish her question.

Miss Barnsley did for her. "Said anything about you? All I know is that he has stood by your innocence, never once claiming to have been *seduced* or *distracted* by you. He always refutes any statements against your properness." That lifted Isabella's heart a small bit. "I think in all honesty... He's ashamed at his own cowardice, that he didn't do more to keep you here. He... He walks like one who's had his spine all crumpled. Doesn't come downstairs anymore. Simply comes in, does his duty as a tutor, and heads off."

"I wish..." *He'd come to see me.* Isabella didn't finish her thought out loud. It didn't matter now. The fact was he hadn't. On top of that, he wasn't anywhere near this house, and hadn't been all day. Isabella had been waiting around for no one.

"Thank you, Miss Barnsley. I better be getting home now." Isabella turned, utterly defeated.

"What's that?" Miss Barnsley pointed to the magazine in Isabella's hand.

"Nothing." Isabella kept on walking. "I hope all are well in the household."

Miss Barnsley didn't respond for a moment, and Isabella wondered if she had already headed back inside, but finally she said, lifting her voice to reach Isabella who was now at the end of the road. "Get home safe, my dear Isabella. I hope things start to look up soon."

Isabella turned and nodded in thanks, but didn't reply. Things didn't seem like they would be looking up in any way anytime soon.

CHAPTER 23

It was with feet of lead that Isabella finally reached the doorstep of her home — Aunt Maggie's home that she had returned to. She rubbed her eyes in an attempt to keep them open, before slowly creaking the door open. It was so late, and she didn't want to disturb Aunt Maggie who surely would already be asleep by now.

But her Aunt wasn't asleep. As Isabella tip-toed into the house, she quickly realised a candle was still burning in the kitchen. Maggie was sitting at the table with someone else, talking in hushed tones. Isabella stepped into the room, allowing her presence to be discovered.

Her Aunt jumped up and pulled Isabella into a hug. "Oh Izzy! I've been worried sick about you. When you didn't come home, and it's so late."

"I'm sorry, Auntie." Isabella said. "I... It's been rather an odd evening. I didn't realise you would have company."

The stranger turned around as they stood up: it was Oliver.

"Miss Farmerson, I apologise if I am intruding in any way."

"Miss Farmerson?" Isabella asked confused. He didn't call

her that anymore. She remembered the shame Miss Barnsley had mentioned, perhaps this was another symptom of it.

"Mr Guildman has been for quite a while waiting for you." Her Aunt explained. "Very charming young man. Even more intelligent than you told me."

Isabella blushed, as did Oliver. Her Aunt continued. "You must be freezing and exhausted, my dear. Sit down, sit down. I'll make you some tea and soup."

Isabella was too exhausted to argue, and too confused and intrigued by Oliver's being here.

"Miss Farmerson I-" Oliver began as Isabella sat down opposite him at the table.

"Isabella. Is still just as fine as it was before." Isabella said. "It was not you who got me cast out, and it was not your fight to have me remain. I hear you have never conceded to join in with dragging my name through the mud, and for that I thank you."

Oliver hung his head. "I should have done more... I felt awful, and still do. Every day I chide myself for not doing... I don't know. But then this morning, this came." Oliver pushed the magazine that had been sitting in front of him over to Isabella. It was the same issue that she had found on the street, though a good deal cleaner.

Isabella pulled out her copy, and put it on top of his. "I know. I found one myself."

"And I'm assuming you've seen the story on page twelve?"

Isabella nodded.

"I instantly recognised your voice in it." Oliver continued. "Your writing style. When I checked to see who had written it, I was even more certain. Arthur could never write anything like this. It was the final straw for me. I couldn't let them take your work, your dream away from you. So I took the day off to come and find you. Tracked down your Aunt and have been waiting here. Your Aunt is an incredible woman, I can see where you get your spirit and sharp wit from."

"Oh, stop you charmer." Aunt Maggie said amused, as she placed a warm bowl of soup and a steaming cup of tea in front of Isabella. "Eat and drink up."

Isabella wasn't sure whether it was the hot food and drink, or Oliver's care for her that warmed her more, but her chest was now buzzing with a nice fuzz. The exhaustion was still there, but it wasn't battling against her anymore.

"It's dastardly, what this impudent child has done." Aunt Maggie said, almost to herself.

"There's nothing that can be done though." Isabella said in despair.

"I wouldn't be so sure of that." Oliver said. "I've had some time to think about it, and I might have a plan."

"A plan?" Isabella asked. "But no one is going to believe a cleaning maid wrote something over the word of a wealthy business man."

"Not unless we can prove it." Oliver said, the determination clear in his voice. "At the very top. Tomorrow morning, we go to the publishers. We go to Bentley's Miscellany and we plead your case. We get you justice."

"You would do this for me?" Isabella asked in disbelief, but very touched. "What will Mr Pennington think?"

"I don't care what Mr Pennington thinks." Oliver said, clenching and unclenching his jaw. "I missed my chance to do right by you before, I won't again. If Mr Pennington has an issue with seeking the truth, then he's not a man I want to work for anyway."

"How exciting." Aunt Maggie said. "I've not witnessed a good shake down in a while. It will be exhilarating, Izzy. We'll be like the heroes in our stories. The three swashbuckling cavillers, making sure that justice is served, and those above follow the same laws as those below."

"I don't know how much swashbuckling will be done, Miss Bloom." Oliver chuckled. "But I know it's the right thing to do. I promise you, Isabella, we will make sure that your story lives on with your name, not branded with a thief's."

Somehow, Isabella completely believed him. She was sure Oliver would stop at nothing to get her story back, and with her formidable Aunt Maggie at his side, it was the poor publisher — who didn't know what was coming for them — that she felt sorry for.

CHAPTER 24

Oliver had taken his leave shortly afterwards, to allow for Isabella and her Aunt to rest up. Isabella was sure she would never be able to sleep, but the second her head hit the pillow, the exhaustion came careening back and she slept like a stone, but with a smile on her face.

The next morning, Oliver met them early and they walked to the Bentley's Miscellany headquarters. It was surprisingly near the paper mill Isabella had been working at, but that made sense really; those printing presses would have to be filled with paper from somewhere.

She would get in trouble for missing a shift at the mill, but if things went well, perhaps Isabella would never have to return to that horrible place ever again. She kept her head down as they walked passed it though, just in case. Her only regret if she never returned there, was that she never solved the mystery of the unknown observer. *Life isn't like the stories.*

The trio arrived at the entrance to the large factory building that had a sign painted in a beautiful red above its large doors.

'BENTLEY'S MISCELLANY
Founded by Richard Bentley 1836'

ISABELLA GASPED. It was here that her favourite magazine was brought to life, and they were about to step inside.

Oliver approached the doorman and whispered something Isabella couldn't quite catch. The doorman glance at Isabella, looking her up and down, and then at Aunt Maggie. Aunt Maggie's life seemed to have been rejuvenated with all the excitement; she hadn't coughed once this morning.

After a tense moment, the doorman nodded at Oliver conspiratorially, and nodded to a second smaller door just off to the right of the immense main ones. Oliver nodded in thanks, and motioned for Isabella and Aunt Maggie to follow him, as they slipped through this side door and into the building.

"What was that?" Isabella whispered to Oliver.

"I called in a favour." Oliver winked at her. "I have some connections in the literary world, humble teacher though I may be."

Isabella smiled. She could practically feel Aunt Maggie buzzing with enjoyment.

"Just like in a story." Her Aunt muttered to herself.

Oliver quickly led them through the large building. They had entered into what must have been the main factory floor. Printing press after printing press was lined up, churning away. It was breathtaking. The smell of ink and almost burning paper filled the air.

"This way." Oliver said, and headed up a flight of stairs. Aunt Maggie raised her eyebrows at Isabella and they followed.

On the upper level there was a section walled off from the noisy factory — where the offices of the administrators must be.

They approached a room that had the name 'Richard Bentley' engraved on the front.

Oliver hesitated before knocking. "Here goes nothing." He knocked.

There was no answer.

He frowned, and knocked again.

"Who is it?" A voice came from inside. Isabella didn't know whether it was Mr Bentley's or not.

"Mr Bentley? I'm here in regards to a story that was published in the latest issue. I don't want to be rash, but I believe a gross case of plagiarism has occurred."

The door swung open, and Oliver instinctively took a step back.

A thin spindly man with round glasses that sat on the brim of his nose stood in the doorway. "Plagiarism? How dare you accuse us of such a thing!"

"Now now good sir." Oliver said, clearly taken aback. "I want't accusing your company or you particularly of- ah… Well…"

"Gentlemen." Aunt Maggie stepped in. Isabella already recognised her tone of voice. It was the same she had used when fighting for custody of Isabella with Miss Strawson. "The young man said he wished not to be rash, lets ourselves also hold to that same standard, shall we? Firstly, I do not believe making accusations in a doorway is ever a good choice, unless one is hoping to get a chamber pot thrown in their face." Aunt Maggie chuckled, and let herself into the room. The spindly gentleman seemed too stunned to stop her. "But I'm sure we don't want any chamberpots being chucked around do we? Especially not where all this paper is concerned."

"No. We most certainly do not." Aunt Maggie received this reply from a man sitting behind the desk in the back middle corner of the room. Oliver and Isabella cautiously but quickly followed Maggie in. The gentlemen that had spoken had to be Richard Bentley. He was a slightly portly man, with an inquisitive face, and a perfectly styled cravat. The main reason Isabella had deduced he was Mr Bentley, however, was that his name was presented on a plaque at the front of his desk. Of the handful of gentlemen that were sitting around the room, he was the one they were looking for.

"And who might you be, most charming madame?" Mr Bentley continued.

"I'm glad you find me charming, Mr…" Aunt Maggie was purposefully making him tell her his name.

He took the bait with a knowing smile. "Mr Bentley. Richard Bentley. Of Bentley's Miscellany."

"Wonderful. So you're the man in charge, and exactly the man we're looking for." Aunt Maggie said. "As for me. I'm Miss Bloom. Miss Maggie Bloom. Magnolia if we're wanting to be fine and proper, but when has the world ever been that." She smirked. "Mr Bentley, this fine young gentleman is Mr Oliver Guildman, and this wonderful young woman is Miss Isabella Farmerson, my niece. And she is the one the matter of plagiarism touches most, for it was her work that has been plagiarised." Aunt Maggie raised her hand as the spindly gentleman tried to speak again. "And before anything else is said, it must be stated, that none of us believe your very reputable and may I say impressively readable magazine ever knowingly participated in this treacherous act, for you too have had the cloak of deception pulled over your face."

Even Oliver raised his eyebrows in surprise. The spindly gentlemen scoffed, and Mr Bentley let out something akin to an impressed whistle. Isabella just smiled — that was Aunt Maggie for you.

"Do you write at all, Miss Bloom?" Mr Bentley asked, a tinge of amusement in his voice.

"I dabble." Aunt Maggie matched his tone. "It is my niece

who is the real writer, and you obviously agree with me, though you do not know it."

"And why do you say that?" The spindly gentleman took on a defensive tone.

"Now now, William. Let's here these people out." Mr Bentley said.

"I say that, Mr…"

"Ainsworth. William Ainsworth."

"I say that, Mr Ainsworth, because you have already published her work. Though it was submitted by someone else. A thief. Mr Guildman, if you would like to explain."

Oliver stepped forward, and nodded slightly awkwardly. Isabella understood, her Aunt could be a tough act to follow. He soon got into the swing of things, though, as he explained the situation: how he and Isabella had met, how they had started working together in the evenings developing each other's skills, and how his student Arthur had framed Isabella and stolen her work for his own.

All the gentlemen followed Mr Bentley's lead, and listened dutifully. Mr Bentley only interrupted once or twice to ask clarification on things.

They're listening. Isabella couldn't believe it. *We might actually have a chance here.*

"That's a very compelling story Mr Guildman and Miss Farmerson." Mr Ainsworth said. "But I am unsure what you want us to do. We can't simply revoke someone's authorship and pull a chapter out of our magazine because of a story. We need proof."

"Well it's clear to me what we need to do, William." Mr Bentley said.

"It is?" Oliver asked, only slightly masking his confusion. Isabella was with him, she didn't think it was very clear what they should do now either.

"We call up this Master Author Pennington, and we hash this

out, as academics." Mr Bentley's mouth curled slightly at the side. He was finding this all rather exciting. The drama was half the reason he'd gotten into publishing in the first place.

"That sounds like an excellent idea." Aunt Maggie interjected. "Call up Master Pennington and his father, and we shall see who's penmanship stands the test."

"Such a way with words, Miss Bloom." Mr Bentley said, as he motioned to one of the gentlemen. "John, would you be willing to go and see about getting the Penningtons here."

"When shall I call them for?" John stood up and adjusted his waistcoat.

Mr Bentley glanced over at Isabella. "Well if you are happy to wait, I'd say call them for as soon as possible. Within the hour or so."

Isabella nodded. "We can wait."

"Jolly good." Mr Bentley smiled. "As soon as possible, John. Thank you."

John nodded and headed out swiftly. A strange moment of calmness came over the room. Finally people were able to catch their breath.

"Begging your pardon, sirs." Isabella couldn't help herself. "But which one of you is Charles Dickens?"

A chuckle rippled around the room, much to Isabella's confusion. She was sure he must have been there — he had written the magazine's best story.

"Charlie isn't here anymore, Miss Farmerson." Mr Bentley said. "The two of us had a bit of a falling out, one could say."

"Oh. I'm very sorry to hear that. I did very much love his story about Oliver Twist."

"A lot of people did." Mr Bentley said. "One of our most profitable. But you know how success makes people. What was it he called me the last time we spoke, William?"

"A Burlington Street Brigand, I believe." This was the first time Isabella had seen Mr Ainsworth show any sort of smile.

"Ah yes! That was it." Mr Bentley shrugged. "You know how we writers are. It's getting a little crowded in here, and will only become more so once the Pennington's show up. May I suggest you go and wait in our meeting room down the hall? We'll join you once the others arrive."

"Thank you very much, sir." Isabella nodded in thanks. Aunt Maggie gave Mr Bentley a smile.

Oliver was very quiet, staring at a spot on the floor, clearly very much in thought. He remained much the same way as they were led down the hall and let into the meeting room. It was a bigger space than Mr Bentley's office, with two large round tables in it. Oliver came to sit at one of them, and seemed to be tracing something in the dust that had settled on the table's surface.

There was a large window that overlooked the factory floor below, and the muffled sound of the presses churning away filled the room with an ambience of work, of progress. Aunt Maggie went over to the window and glanced down at the large expanse of machinery.

"Are you okay?" Isabella came to sit down next to Oliver.

"I'm fine. Better even." Oliver replied, whilst continuing to trace, in the dust. Isabella wasn't sure whether he was actually writing or drawing something, or simple keeping his fingers busy. "We've gotten a lot further a lot quicker than I expected."

"That's my Aunt for you." Isabella shot a look over at Aunt Maggie, who winked back at her. "She never was one to wait around for things. She always made them happen."

"I just thought I'd have more time to formulate a plan." Oliver forced a small grin. "We've made a serious accusation. We've got to make sure we prove it now, for all our sakes."

"What are you thinking?" Isabella asked, the weight of the situation started to settle in now that the excitement was passing.

"It's still coming together, but I'm thinking we do it the old-fashioned way. We sit you both down, and we have you write something. I then compare the syntax of each to the published story in the magazine, and that should prove the story is yours. You both have such different styles, and don't believe Arthur would have been able to completely learn your style, let alone reproduce it under pressure."

"I've never had to write under pressure before either though..." Isabella said.

"Yes you have." Aunt Maggie retorted, as she came away from the window to join them. "Every time you came up with a story as you verbally told it, that was you writing under pressure. You didn't 'um' and 'ah' while you sat telling your friends at the orphanage stories did you? The words just came naturally and they flowed."

"Orphanage?" Oliver asked.

"I'll tell another time." Isabella said. "A story for another day."

Oliver nodded in understanding. "All you need to do Isabella, is be your wonderful smart self, and all shall be put right. I promise you."

He took Isabella's hand, and gave it a comforting squeeze.

All shall be put right.

CHAPTER 25

It turned out that John was very good at his job, and the Pennington's arrived a mere hour and a half later. Arthur was practically dragged in by his father, who looked like he also didn't want to be there, but more because of anger than any sort of shame. The only Pennington that looked happy to have been summoned was Lola, she had come along as soon as she had overheard what the issue was.

"I demanded to come." She whispered to Isabella as everyone was shuffling into seats. "I've missed you."

"I've missed you too." Isabella said with a smile.

"I know that Arthur stole your work." Lola said. "And I know that you and Mr Guildman will be able to prove it."

"Lola!" Mr Pennington called. "Stop talking to that maid and come and sit by me."

Lola looked like she wanted to say more to Isabella, but held her tongue. She dutifully went over to her step-father and sat down.

"Now." Mr Pennington lifted his voice to command the room. "What is it exactly that you are accusing my son of, Mr Bentley?"

"I am not accusing him of anything, Mr Pennington." Mr Bentley kept his voice calm and level. "It has been brought to my attention that there is a possibility that your son, Master Arthur Pennington, stole the story that he submitted to our magazine. We take plagiarism very seriously here at Bentley's Miscellany you see."

Mr Pennington scoffed in incredulous disbelief. "My son? A thief! How dare you say such a thing. Why I aught to—" Mr Pennington cut himself off, and jabbed a finger at Oliver. "Mr Guildman, how dare you do such a thing as this?"

"How dare your son do such a thing." Oliver stood his ground.

"Now gentlemen." Oliver stood up to address the entire room. All of the gentlemen who had been assembled in the office had come to attend, as well as a few more. This was the most exciting thing that had happened at this place since Mr Dickens stormed out. "I do comprehend the weight of the accusation, and do not wish to simply make it without any proof. Baseless words are useless. Now you each have in front of you a copy of the magazine with the story in question. I'm assuming you've all had a chance to read it?" He turned to Arthur. "Have you read it, Arthur?"

"Well, yes, of course I have!" Arthur stammered. "I wrote it after all. It says right there." He jabbed his finger onto the paper.

"Writers have styles, have voices. We can hear them in their words, can't we?" A murmur of agreements.

"Can you get on with it, Mr Guildman?" Mr Pennington complained. "I've had quite enough of your bravado and fancy words. What is it that you require of my son to prove his innocence? Come to a point. Now."

"I shall jump to the point, Mr Pennington." Oliver set a pen and piece of paper in front of both Arthur and Isabella. "I propose we have both our potential authors do what they do best, write. Let's have them write something short, nothing more than a page or two should be necessary, with which we can then cross reference with the published story. The style that fits, the voice that matches up the most, we can conclude is the real author of this piece. Do you agree, Mr Bentley?"

Mr Bentley took in a long deep breath of deliberation before responding: "I agree, Mr Guildman. Let us have them write."

Isabella felt her breath catch in her throat. She was going to have to do this. A quick look at Oliver helped to calm her nerves. His warm eyes were looking at her with nothing but adoration and respect.

"Do you agree to this experiment, Miss Farmerson?" Oliver asked.

"I do." Isabella nodded.

"And do you agree, Master Pennington?"

"This is utter rubbish!" Arthur cried out. "She's nothing but a maid! She couldn't have written any of this, it's clear! Can't we all just go home!"

"If you do not agree, Master Pennington." Mr Bentley's voice took a sharp edge. "I shall have your name removed from the story automatically, and a letter explaining that you do not represent the values of the magazine, regardless as to whether or not you wrote the thing. Do you understand me, boy?"

"How dare you talk to my son that way!" Mr Pennington stood up in outrage.

Mr Bentley stayed sitting. "I talk to him as I would an uncooperative business partner, Mr Pennington, since that is what he is. I'm sure you understand yourself."

Mr Pennington's face was starting to go red with fury, but he did not respond to Mr Bentley, instead he turned to Oliver. "My son agrees. Have them write their silly little paper and be done with it." He sat down heavily, and gave Arthur a grave look.

Arthur looked sick, and Isabella began to feel sorry for him a small amount; he surely hadn't expected to end up here when he had stolen her work, and entertained the idea of being regarded as a skilled writer, lauded in a prestigious magazine.

"Very well." Oliver nodded. "Mr Bentley, would you do us the honour of giving our writers their stimulus? The thing they shall write about for us?"

Mr Bentley stroked his chin. "A great honour, Mr Guildman, to have one's ideas brought to life by a writer's words..." He took another moment thinking, basking in the dramatics of it all. "I would like you both to write me a short story about a boy with a toffee apple, which is stolen by a dog." He smiled to himself, satisfied with the scenario he had come up with. "Simply and sweet. Like a toffee apple."

"A lovely choice, sir." Oliver turned to Arthur and Isabella, who were both sitting with the pen's in their hands, one sat on each table. "Writers, you may begin when you please. You shall have... Shall we say thirty minutes?"

Mr Pennington looked like he was about to cry out in protest again, but Mr Ainsworth jumped in first. "Thirty minutes sounds like a fine amount of time, young man."

"Thirty minutes then." Oliver repeated. "May we come to a conclusion to this matter."

CHAPTER 26

Isabella put down her pen. She was finished. When she had begun writing, it felt like she was having to push her pen through thick treacle, nothing was coming to her, but as she went on it became easier; the world of the story became more tangible, and she found herself even enjoying it. This is what God designed her to do: write.

She sat back in her seat, to make it clear she was finished. She wasn't sure how long was left of the allotted time, but a quick glance over to Arthur let her know he was still frantically scribbling away. Isabella had been tempted to try and overwrite her piece — show off all the techniques she knew — but that had the possibility of backfiring. She had made sure her book was written efficiently, and so she aimed for that same precision with this short story. It wasn't her finest work, but considering the circumstances, she felt proud of it.

Making eye contact with Oliver, she let herself smile a little. She could breathe again. There was nothing more she could do now, it was up to Oliver to point out the similarities and differences.

"Times up Master Pennington." Mr Ainsworth said, glancing at his pocket watch. "Pen down please."

"What about--" Arthur stopped himself. He had been so focussed on his own writing, he hadn't noticed that Isabella had her pen sitting above her piece of paper and was leaning back in her chair, arms at her side. "All right. Al lright... I didn't get time to quite finish it, but, there it is. Whatever." He dropped the pen disrespectfully onto the page. A small ink blot appeared where it landed.

"Mr Guildman." Mr Bentley said. "May I suggest sending out anyone who won't be involved in the deliberation? Just to free up the room, and allow us to be the most efficient with our time." It wasn't clear who Mr Bentley was directing his comments towards, but Mr Pennington clearly felt an offence at them.

Oliver glanced at Isabella, she nodded at him. "Of course, sir. Shall they just wait in the hallway? This shouldn't take long."

"Miss Bloom. Mr and Master Pennington. Miss Pennington. Miss Farmerson. If you wouldn't mind?" Mr Bentley looked and nodded at each person as he addressed them.

Mr Pennington looked as if he was about to protest, but when Arthur simply stood and started walking out, he shut his mouth and left the room too.

Isabella squeezed Oliver's hand as she walked out. "Good luck."

"With your skill, I won't need it." He whispered.

～

THE AIR in the hallway was tense. Aunt Maggie sat sewing a small piece of her blouse back together. She had been meaning to mend it for ages, and now was finally a time to do it.

Lola sat, only risking a glance or two at Isabella, always with a smile. Arthur just sat staring down at the floor. All fight had seemingly left him.

Mr Pennington walked over and towered above Isabella. "Why are you doing this? Do you think I want to be here? Why do you insist on using the people you have seduced to continue to torment my son?"

"I'm not tormenting your son, sir." Isabella held her ground, staring back up at Mr Pennington. "I am simply wanting to receive credit for the work I have done. And your son needs to learn, he cannot just take from this world without a single regard for anyone else. You of all people should know that, Mr Pennington. The world is already so unfair, we must strive to bring fairness back into it, not partake in the depravity." Her words left Mr Pennington speechless, and he went and sat down beside his son and step-daughter.

They waited in silence.

Oliver's muffled voice vibrated from behind the closed door. Isabella couldn't make out what he was saying, but his rhythm was consistent and confident. She had total trust in him.

After about ten minutes of waiting, which had felt like ten hours, the door was opened by Mr Ainsworth, and he invited them back in.

The five of them retook their seats in silence, waiting to hear the verdict.

Oliver was sittinng with his head in his hands. That wasn't a good sign.

Mr Bentley cleared his throat before starting. "Today has been an especially exciting one, and I did truly mean it when I said it was an honour to have writers bring my ideas to life. Upon reviewing the two tales against the piece in the magazine, the evidence is compelling, but we as a collective just can't make a decision based wholly on something so objective."

Isabella felt like someone had punched her in the chest. She crumpled into her chair. This was it, everything was going to crumble around her. Again.

"I'm sorry Miss Farmerson. And I am sorry to you Mr Pennington for taking time out of your day."

"But in conclusion?" Mr Pennington demanded.

"In conclusion..." Mr Bentley said, casting an ashamed look towards Isabella. "Nothing is to be done or changed."

Nothing would be done or changed...

Arthur sat almost in shock. He had somehow gotten away with it.

"Unless something more solid can be presented."

Oliver let out a laugh. This surprised everyone in the room, most of all him. "How could I have missed it?" He said, almost to himself.

"I'm sorry, Mr Guildman?" Mr Bentley asked.

Oliver jumped up. "It's so simple. I've been going about this as a twelve-step problem when really it's only two." He rushed round the table, and picked up the two newly written pieces. He studied both of them for a moment, and then nodded to himself. "Do you have the original manuscript for the story?" Oliver asked Mr Bentley.

"No. Master Pennington retained that." Mr Bentley said.

"Have you brought it with you?" Oliver turned and asked Mr Pennington.

"Of course not!" Mr Pennington burst out. "That's kept safe at home, and it won't be brought out, if that's what you're asking. I've had enough of this."

"I've brought it." Lola spoke up. "I have the original manuscript here with me." She pulled out what Isabella recognised to be her own book. "Here it is."

"Where did you get that?" Arthur demanded. "That was in my desk."

"I know." Lola looked her stepbrother dead in the eye. "I also knew you never would have brought it today, so I made sure to pack it before we left."

"You little—"

"Stop Arthur." Mr Pennington put a hand on his son's shoulder. "Well… As it's here. Do as you will Mr Guildman's. Just let us all go home soon."

"This will be even more rapid, Mr Pennington, I assure you." Oliver held his hand out to Lola for the book. "May I, Miss Pennington?" Lola gladly handed him the book.

He placed it down in the middle of the table, clearly in view for Mr Pennington, and he flipped it open to a random page. He then placed both pieces of new work either side of the book.

"Look at the 'Q's, at the 'W's, even the 'S's. It's so clear, isn't it. Of these two works, which hand *literally* matches? The handwriting of one clearly lines up, whilst the other does not."

"Miss Farmerson…" Mr Bentley said quietly. "It seems we owe you an apology." He looked up at her and stretched his hand out to shake hers.

Isabella rose, and took Mr Bentley's hand and shook it. "Thank you, Mr Bentley."

"We must discuss how we plan to continue publishing the story in our magazine. There is a couple of things we will need to discuss and decide on, especially with you being a woman." Mr Bentley cleared his throat. "However, I do hope you would like to continue with us?" Mr Bentley said.

"Of course I would!" Isabella did her best not to raise her voice in excitement. "I have been an avid follower of the magazine for years."

"That is wonderful to hear." Mr Bentley smiled.

Mr Pennington stood up in silence, practically dragged Arthur up, and started leaving the room without a word. As he passed Oliver he paused: "I hope you know this means you are never coming back to work for me."

"I understand, sir. I hope you find Arthur a good replacement tutor."

Mr Pennington gave Isabella a look that she couldn't quite decipher. It held within it anger, shame, understanding, and even a hint of respect. He was an enigma of a man, one who probably was good deep down, but had let the world of business and money corrupt him. "Come, Lola. We're leaving." He walked out the door without waiting for her to follow.

Lola quickly approached Isabella and gave her a big hug. "Congratulations Isabella!"

"Thank you, Lola! For standing up for me, and for…" Isabella glanced at the door Mr and Master Pennington had just walked out of. "Will you be okay? You defied Mr Pennington."

"I'll be fine." Lola said determined. "I did what was right. Father already knows that in his heart, and he'll come to accept it. I hope I'll see you again someday."

"I'm sure you will! Us storytellers always end up running into each other." Isabella gave Lola another hug, before she quickly left to follow her stepfather and brother.

Isabella turned to Oliver, and embraced him. "Thank you so much!" She pulled out of the hug. "I'm so sorry I got you fired. I'm sure if we—"

"Isabella, there's no need to apologise. I wouldn't want to be around people that disrespected you. Because…" Oliver hesitated.

In the corner of her eye, Isabella spotted Aunt Maggie raise her eyebrow, and quickly move over to Mr Bentley to congratulate him on a job well done, and distract him for a short time to give her and Oliver a moment alone.

"Because?" Isabella asked.

"Because I love, Isabella." Oliver said. "I love your mind, your heart, your stories. I want to spend the rest of my life hearing them. I want to be a part of your story, if you'll have me. Miss Isabella Farmerson, will you marry me?"

"Yes!" Isabella cried out in glee, she jumped forward and kissed Oliver. He laughed in surprise, but quickly kissed her back. It was the most incredible feeling she had ever felt. Finally, things all clicked into place. Finally, she was getting her happy ending.

She pulled away. Not everything was quite resolved yet. There was one more thing she needed to make right.

"Mr Bentley." She turned to the publisher. "Do you mind if we return tomorrow to discuss the continuation of the publication of my story? Today's been rather dramatic already as you can see. I've just been proposed to, and I have something very important to attend to."

"Of course, Miss Farmerson!" Mr Bentley chuckled. "With how things have gone so far, we owe you a day's respite at least."

"Thank you dearly, sir." She turned back to Oliver. "There's one more thing I must set right before I can have my happily ever after. Will you come with me?"

"Of course." Oliver said, holding her face gently in his hands. "I would follow you anywhere."

CHAPTER 27

Isabella knocked again. There hadn't been an answer the first two times, but she was determined. A light rain had started to fall, and Oliver stood covering his head with his hands. Aunt Maggie had stayed behind to discuss the prospect of working with Mr Bentley herself too.

"Where is this?" Oliver asked.

"This is the orphanage I spent a year of my life in." Isabella responded without looking away from the door. Maybe if she just focussed hard enough it would open. "There was a girl there named Nancy. She looked after me, was my closest friend. I promised her I would come back for her, and now that my life is settling in—" She did turn and smile at Oliver as she said that. "It feels like the right time to find her."

Isabella's heart leaped as there was the clunk of a lock being lifted on the inside of the door. It creaked open a few inches, and an older but unforgettable face peered out at Isabella.

It was Miss Strawson. Her face had gotten more gaunt, and she seemed slightly shorter — but it was unmistakably her.

"What do you want?" She squawked. "Meetings must be prearranged, no walk-ins!"

"Miss Strawson! It's me. Miss Isabella Farmerson." Isabella exclaimed. "I stayed here for a time, quite a few years ago now."

Miss Strawson peered up at Isabella's face and scrunched her eyebrows. "No. No, sorry. Don't know you. Goodbye."

She began to close the door, but Isabella caught it with her foot. "Miss Strawson. Please. I'm looking for someone. Nancy. She was here with me. We were an inseparable duo. Please remember. Please."

"If she was here with you..." Miss Strawson half muttered. "She won't be here anymore. At eighteen, all girls must leave, and you are definitely older than eighteen. I can't help you. Good day." Miss Strawson moved Isabella's foot out of the way of the door with a cane Isabella hadn't noticed, and shut it. Isabella's heart sank as she heard the lock fall back into place.

"She was charming." Oliver said, trying to lighten the mood. He looked over at Isabella, who didn't respond. Gently, he lifted her head up with his hand. "We'll find her, I promise."

"She could be anywhere." Isabella said, crestfallen. "I don't even know if she's alive anymore. These streets are so rough, especially to..." Isabella trailed off, as things began connecting in her mind. All of the dramatics with the magazine had made Isabella forget what she had been waiting, outside the paper mill, for in the first place, but now...

"What?" Oliver recognised Isabella's expression as one of rapid thought.

Isabella let out a laugh. "But it can't be that easy! That would only happen in a story!"

"What?" Oliver asked again, but laughing along with Isabella.

"Quick." Isabella grabbed Oliver's hand. "It's almost the end of the work day. If we run, we'll make it."

The two sprinted down the street hand in hand.

"Where are we going?" Oliver asked.

"To the paper mill!"

CHAPTER 28

They sprinted hard, and did make it to the paper mill just as the work day was coming to a close. Droves of workers were exiting and shuffling off to their homes. It was much the same as the last time Isabella had been waiting to try and find the mystery woman — but this time she knew her name.

"Nancy!" Isabella called out. She got a few surprised and sour looks from the tired workers, but no response. She called again. "Nancy!"

Oliver joined in. "Nancy! Is a Nancy here?"

Isabella started rushing through the crowd, asking people as she zig-zagged between them. "I'm looking for Nancy? Do any of you know a Nancy? About my height. Shorter hair. Works here." Some people wouldn't meet her eyes, others simply shook their heads.

The crowd was starting to thin, and Isabella once again was losing hope. What if she had been wrong? After all, it would have been too kind of a coincidence, wouldn't it? If she was right though, how incredible that the two girls had come so close to crossing paths again after all these years.

"You weren't here today." A voice said from behind Isabella. "But don't worry, I didn't snitch. The foreman's just like Miss Strawson was."

Isabella spun round. There she was — Nancy.

"Hi." Nancy said with a smile. "It's been awhile."

It was strange, because obviously she looked older, she was taller and her hair was a darker shade than before though she had still kept it short, but Isabella instantly recognised her. Their bond was something deeper. She rushed forward and pulled Nancy into a hug. She held on tight. For the first time, a world that had been ripped away from Isabella was in her grasp again, she was able to take some control. For the first time, Isabella was able to return to someone she'd lost.

"I told you I was coming back." Isabella said, still not letting go. "I'm sorry it took me so long."

"You don't need to be sorry for anything!" Nancy said, starting to cry. "It just means we'll have plenty to tell each other now. Our story has a lot to catch up with."

Isabella laughed through her own tears. It was just like the old days. The two of them, just young orphans, against the world, bringing brightness to it through stories.

"And how's this?" Nancy said, with her unmistakable mischief. "You have been busy without me." She raised an eyebrow at Oliver.

"Hello." Oliver stepped forward and extended a hand. "My name is Mr Oliver Guildman, but my friends call me Oliver, so you can too. Any friend of Isabella's is a friend of mine."

"I like him already." Nancy quipped to Isabella. "Well I'm Nancy. Just Nancy."

"Lovely to meet you, Nancy." Oliver smiled at seeing his fiancé so overjoyed and restored.

"I'm glad you like him." Isabella said, taking Oliver's hand whilst still having an arm wrapped around Nancy. "Because you've just been invited to our wedding."

EPILOGUE

"It really was a beautiful wedding." Isabella said, smiling fondly at the memory from ten years ago. "Nancy was so grateful to be there, and Aunt Maggie was just beside herself. She brought along Mr Bentley as her guest, which was rather amusing." Isabella chuckled.

"And after all that? What has happened?"

"Well, I'm a writer now. I've continued to work with Bentley's Miscellany. My first book was a real success, even with all the initial confusion over the authorship. In fact, my real name isn't even on it now!

"I sat down with Mr Bentley and we discussed it all. He was not sure if people would accept a woman writer, so my stories are being published under a penname. It sounds silly I know, we went through all that because someone else's name was on my story, and then we go ahead and put a different name on it again, but at least this time I chose the name. Oscar Farmerson. My father's name.

"I'm actually currently working on my third novel with them." Isabella said. "But that's not what I'm proudest of. That might have been my dream, and it is truly incredible, and I am so grateful for it, but I've found a new calling as well. I'm also a teacher with my husband. We run a small school for boys and girls who wouldn't get the opportunity to receive any education otherwise. There isn't a lot of money in it, but it is so gratifying." She glanced down at her bag, which was full of papers she still had to grade. "Oliver and I still make sure to work on our own pieces too, when we get the time. He's very romantic about it all."

"That's good. I'm very glad to hear that."

"Aunt Maggie also writes now. It is a much kinder job than cleaning, and it let her recover. She's never been fitter I would say." Isabella laughed, as did the elderly lady lying in bed. They had been speaking for hours now. "Nancy looks after the baby for us when me and Oliver want to work just the two of us."

"Baby?" The lady exclaimed in surprise.

"Yes! We have a beautiful little daughter named Daisy." Isabella placed a hand on her belly. "And another little boy or girl coming soon too."

"Well I'm sure they'll both be bright stars, just like their mother." The lady raised her hand and caressed Isabella's cheek. "I am so so sorry for how I left you. I should have done more."

"No no. We all had our hardships to face back then." Isabella placed her hand on top of the one on her cheek. "I have nothing but love for you. I'm sorry it has taken me this long to find you."

"Thank you for coming. Thank you for finding me. Even if it is just to say goodbye. I am so glad I have gotten the chance to see the beautiful and incredible woman that you have grown to be. Your parents would be so proud. I'm sure they're looking down from Heaven right now, beaming with joy and love."

A tear streaked down Isabella's cheek. "I look forward to seeing them again one day, and being able to tell them all the stories I have."

"I'll let them know. But don't come too soon! You've got plenty more stories to write before then." The lady's eyes started to close, tired but content.

"I won't be too quick." Isabella chuckled. "Thank you again, Mrs Paxton. Sleep well."

THE FIRST CHAPTER OF 'THE LOST ORPHANS OF DARK STREETS'

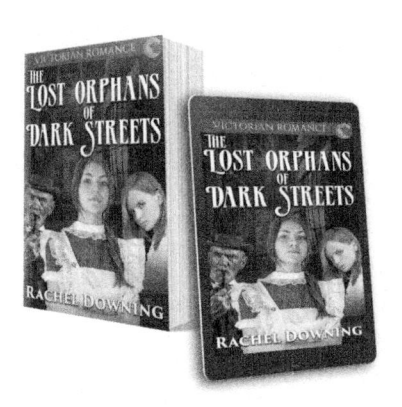

Seven-year-old Elizabeth Green experienced trauma early in life. She grew up living in the apartment above her family's button shop in Birmingham with her mother and father, and although their family kept to themselves and she had no other relatives to speak of, she never felt lonely and always knew she was loved as long as her parents were beside her. Her mother Lily was a gentlehearted woman with a smile for everyone. She regarded even the rudest of customers at the button shop with empathy, imagining the difficulties they must have been enduring to upset them so much, and telling Elizabeth that she should always look for the best in people, and forgive them their mistakes.

Her father Samuel was generally a quiet, hardworking man, but he offered his family a steady sort of love and care that never left any room to doubt his devotion to them.

Elizabeth took after both her parents in her own way. She was a quiet child, too, preferring to hum songs to herself over going outside to find others to play with, but she was curious too, and she listened to every word spoken in her presence with a careful consideration that suggested she never planned to forget a single thing she had heard. Life in a button shop was not what most people would consider glamorous, but the buttons were like jewels to Elizabeth's eyes, a sparkling, multi-coloured treasure that she got to play with every day. She loved seeing fancy people's clothes, when they brought in their gowns and jackets for their buttons to be replaced, and she loved sitting beside her mother as she taught her how to mend a tear so that you couldn't see a single stitch, or to reattach a button so that it would never fall off again.

"But don't we want it to fall off?" Elizabeth had asked her. "Otherwise they won't come back."

"We want to be as good as we can to our customers," her mother said patiently. "It would be wrong to do a poor job to force them to spend more money. And besides, if our buttons always fall off, they'll go elsewhere. If our buttons are steady and trustworthy, like we aim to be, they'll always come back when they need something new."

Elizabeth also loved seeing her father at work, so focussed and peaceful looking, with a glint in his eye that told the world how much pride he took in his craft. She was not allowed to help make any of the buttons, for her father was a perfectionist in his work and he thought Elizabeth far too young, but she loved to watch her father and see the proud little smile that would gently spread across his face when he finished a job well done.

But one day, Elizabeth's mother went out in the early evening to deliver some completed work to a customer and did not return. Elizabeth waited up for her in the front of the shop while her father worked on a few more orders, watching the lamplighter pass by with his work and the streets gradually darken as night fell. When her father finally looked up from his work, it was fully dark, and her mother was beyond late. It must have been past dinner time, because Elizabeth's stomach growled with hunger, but she continued to sit by the shop window, looking at the now-empty street for any sign of her mother.

"Still not back yet?" her father said as he walked up to stand beside her. He kept his tone mild, but Elizabeth thought she heard a little worry in there, too. She shook her head, and her father sighed. "Maybe she got waylaid," he said. "Mrs. Higgins is the sort of customer who likes to talk. Your mother probably knows about the history and condition of every one of her dogs by now. She'll be home soon."

But her father did not sound convinced. They locked up the shop and headed upstairs, knowing that her mother had a key, but her father refused to eat supper until she was home, leaving Elizabeth to sit by the window, stomach rumbling, watching for any sign of her mother's return.

She nodded off, waiting, and woke up around midnight to her father's gentle hand on her shoulder. "Elizabeth," he murmured. "I'm going out. I'll be back soon."

"Where are you going?" Elizabeth murmured. "Where's mama?"

"She'll be home soon," her father said. "You wait here for her, all right?"

Elizabeth nodded, rubbing the sleep from her eyes, and her father squeezed her shoulder one more time before leaving. Her stomach felt completely empty now, so she took a candle to the kitchen and grabbed a small piece of bread. After thinking for a moment, she walked back downstairs again, where the windows were larger, and she could more easily see her mother's approach.

But another hour passed, exhaustion tugging at Elizabeth's eyelids, and neither her mother nor her father returned. Elizabeth curled up in a ball on her chair, pulling her knees tight to her chest and sucking on her thumb to comfort herself as she waited, and waited. The sun was already rising by the time her father finally re-emerged. He walked with a stagger, and he had to pause for a moment outside the shop, his head down. Then he unlocked the door, and Elizabeth leapt to her feet.

"Where's mama?" she said

Her father shook his head and did not speak.

"Papa," she said. "Wasn't she at Mrs. Higgins's?"

"I don't know where she is, Elizabeth," her father said hoarsely. "There's no sign of her. I looked everywhere, but—"

"Then we have to tell the police!" Elizabeth said. She'd heard lots of stories where people got into trouble, and they all said that the police were the people to help. Her father and mother had taught her that too, while tucking her in at night, telling her that if she ever got lost or hurt and couldn't find her parents, then finding a policeman was the next best thing.

But her father shook his head again. "I've been," he said. "They wouldn't listen."

"What?" Elizabeth asked. That didn't make sense. She'd been taught that the police *always* helped.

Her father ran his hand through his hair. "They said we don't know she's really missing, that she might have just run off, and they can't waste time looking for a missing wife when she probably doesn't *want* to be found." Her father was murmuring almost to himself now. "But she would never run off like this," he said. "She must be in some sort of trouble. But I looked and I looked and—" He looked up suddenly, his eyes falling on Elizabeth again. "Have you seen any sign of her while I was gone? Did she say anything to you?"

Elizabeth shook her head.

"All right," her father said. "All right. Then—then I'd better look for her some more. Go upstairs, Elizabeth, and stay there. Don't open the door to anyone, you understand me?"

"But papa—"

"Go," he said, giving her a gentle push. "I'll be back as soon as I can."

But her father did not return for hours. The sun rose, and Elizabeth sat upstairs with her face against the small window overlooking the street. Customers came to the still-locked door, confused that the store was not open, but her father did not return.

Then, around noon, two policemen walked to the front of the store and knocked.

Ignoring her father's warning, Elizabeth scurried down the stairs and unlocked the door. The policeman looked down at her. "Is your father home?" he asked.

Elizabeth shook her head.

"Is this the residence of Mrs. Lily Green?"

Elizabeth nodded, unable to speak.

"Your mother?" the second policeman asked her, not unkindly. She nodded again. The men glanced at one another, but before they could speak again, Elizabeth's father's voice cut through the street.

"Elizabeth!" he shouted. Elizabeth had never heard him speak so loudly before. She jumped and looked past the policemen to see her father running toward her.

"This is your father?" the first policeman asked her. She nodded as her father reached them and stepped around the policemen to put a hand on her shoulder.

"What's the problem, sirs?" her father asked. He looked pale, with dark circles under his eyes from lack of sleep.

"Mr. Samuel Green?" the first policeman asked. "I am afraid we have some bad news, sir. Perhaps—not in front of the child."

Elizabeth gripped hold of her father's arm. "Is it mama?" she asked, in a quiet voice. "What's happened to mama?"

"Elizabeth, go inside," her father said, but that only caused her to grip hold of his arm tighter. Her father glanced at her, and then all the fight seemed to drop out of him. "What happened?" he asked the policemen.

"She was found by the river this morning, sir," the policeman said.

Elizabeth felt a rush of joy. They'd found her mama! She would be coming home! But then she saw the way her father's face paled even further, and the grave expressions on the policemen's faces, and she thought perhaps she had misunderstood.

"What happened?" her father asked, his voice hoarse.

"We cannot say, sir. Got mixed up with something she shouldn't, most likely."

"No," her father said, shaking his head. "No, that's not her."

"These gangs," the policeman said, "they sometimes use pretty things like her to do their dirty work. Think they'll be able to get away with it easy, because they're women."

"No!" her father said again. "That is not what happened. She was not a criminal. Someone must have attacked her. It's murder."

"I am sorry, sir," the policeman said again. "We thought it best to inform you."

Murder. The word rang through Elizabeth's head. *Murder.* "Mama—mama's dead?" she asked, in a small voice.

Her father tightened his grip on her shoulder and then pushed her inside. "Go upstairs now, Elizabeth," he said. "*Now.*"

He shouted so loudly that Elizabeth found herself obeying before she could think. The world spun around her as she climbed the stairs. None of it felt quite real. Her mama could not be dead. It didn't make any sense.

As soon as she was upstairs, she staggered back to her post by the window, where she could glimpse a little of the policemen's heads and hear some of the argument that drifted up from the street. Her father was shouting at the policemen, telling them that they had to find out who had done this, and the policemen were speaking sternly back to him, almost threatening him now that Elizabeth was gone. They told him if he did not stop arguing, they would investigate him and his business for criminal activity, too.

Elizabeth rested her head on her knees and sobbed.

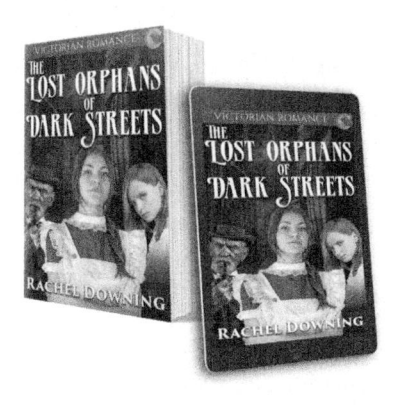

Clear here to read the rest of
'The Lost Orphans of Dark Streets'

GET TWO INCREDIBLE TALES IN ONE!! *Follow the stories of Elizabeth and Molly as they negotiate the dangerous slums and find their place in the world.*

BOOK 1 - THE BUTTON MAKER'S ORPHAN DAUGHTER

Even though she only lives in a button-shop in Liverpool,

Elizabeth Green couldn't be more content. Both her parents are hard workers and are bringing her up to be virtuous, caring, and hard working. But when a strange man, somehow related to her mother, turns up and causes a disruption, Elizabeth's comfortable life could be taken from her forever.

Being kept in the dark about the meaning of this stranger, and intrigued by the young apprentice who he brings with him, Elizabeth's search for the truth gets both herself and her parents in trouble.

Will Elizabeth be able to negotiate the secrets even her father has kept from her? Will she discover the identity of the mysterious gentleman and find a connection with his handsome young apprentice? And can she find answers, all while surviving in the crime-ridden city of Birmingham?

BOOK 2 - THE LOST ORPHAN'S CAUSE

The harsh life of the workhouse is all orphan Molly has ever known. Cruelty and hard work were her school, until the day of her escape.

The loneliness of the workhouse now replaced by the dangers of the dark London streets, the opportunity to run with a gang of vagabonds and urchins at first seems like the family she has never known. But Molly knows there's something more, something just around the corner...

Will Molly be able to find the place she truly belongs? Will she be able to evade being caught by the police and workhouse authorities? And what will she do when a person from her past thrusts her into an unexpected and entirely different world?

OUR GIFT TO YOU

AS A WAY TO SAY THANK YOU WE WOULD LOVE TO SEND YOU THIS BEAUTIFUL STORY FREE OF CHARGE.

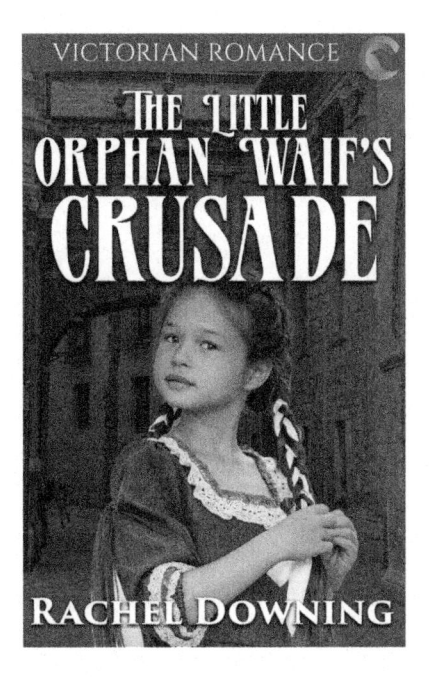

Click here for your FREE COPY of
'The Little Orphan Waif's Crusade'
CornerstoneTales.com/sign-up

In the wake of her father's passing, seven-year-old Matilda is determined to heal her sister Effie's shattered spirit.

Desperate to restore joy to Effie's life, Matilda embarks on a daring quest, aided by the gentle-hearted postman, Philip. Together, they weave a plan to ignite the flame of love in Effie's heart once more.

At Cornerstone Tales we publish books you can trust. Great tales without sex or swearing, but with all of the mystery and romance you expect from a great story.

Be the first to know when we release new books, take part in our fun competitions, and get surprise free books in your inbox by signing up to our free VIP Reader list.

As a thank you you'll receive a copy of 'The Little Orphan Waif's Crusade' straight away, alongside other gifts.

Click here to sign up for our mailing list, and receive your FREE stories.

CornerstoneTales.com/sign-up

LOVE VICTORIAN ROMANCE?

Other Rachel Downing Books

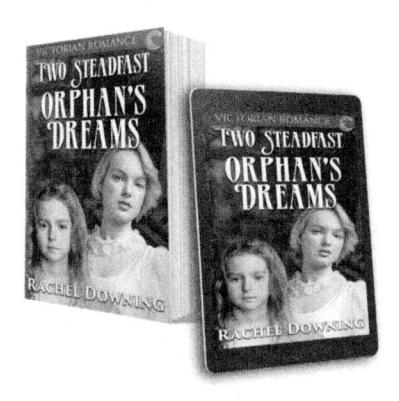

Two Steadfast Orphan's Dreams

Follow the stories of Isabella and Ada as they overcome all odds and find love.

Get 'Two Steadfast Orphan's Dreams' Here!

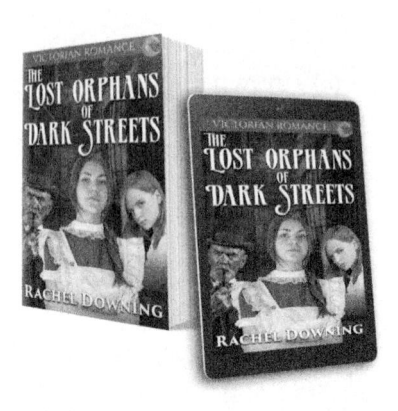

The Lost Orphans of Dark Streets

Follow the stories of Elizabeth and Molly as they negotiate the dangerous slums and find their place in the world.

Get 'The Lost Orphans of Dark Streets' Here!

If you enjoyed this story, sign up to our mailing list to be the first to hear about our new releases and any sales and deals we have.

We also want to offer you a Victorian Romance novella - 'The Little Orphan Waif's Crusade' - absolutely free!

Click here to sign up for our mailing list, and receive your FREE stories.

CornerstoneTales.com/sign-up

Printed in Great Britain
by Amazon